'Moving, thoughtful and absorbing . . .
Alberto's Lost Birthday reminds us of the importance
of home and the peace that comes with
knowing who we truly are'
Mail on Sunday

'A novel that charms and illuminates
in equal measure'
Fanny Blake, *Daily Mail*

'Truly moving . . . A feel-good book with a
difference [and] a page-turner that'll leave a smile on
your face and a warm fuzzy feeling in your heart . . .
The perfect read for holidays or me time for
when the kids are asleep'
Good to Know

'This warming story will capture your heart
until the very end'
Essentials

'Charming . . . A film script surely beckons'
Herald

'A fascinating look at Spain's troubled history
and a heart-warming inter-generational love story
about the bonds of family'
Red

Alberto's Lost Birthday

A copywriter by trade, Diana Rosie has created award-winning campaigns for a variety of popular brands, and occasionally helps her filmmaker husband with script-writing.

After living in Hong Kong, London and Peru, she has finally settled comfortably into a country cottage, where she writes by the range.

Alberto's Lost Birthday is her first novel.

DIANA ROSIE

Alberto's Lost Birthday

PAN BOOKS

First published 2016 by Mantle

This paperback edition published 2016 by Pan Books
an imprint of Pan Macmillan
20 New Wharf Road, London N1 9RR
Associated companies throughout the world
www.panmacmillan.com

ISBN 978-1-4472-9303-3

1 3 5 7 9 8 6 4 2

A CIP catalogue record for this book is available from the British Library.

Printed and bound by CPI Group (UK) Ltd, Croydon, CR0 4YY

Visit www.panmacmillan.com to read more about all our books
and to buy them. You will also find features, author interviews and
news of any author events, and you can sign up for e-newsletters
so that you're always first to hear about our new releases.

For John, who brings me sunshine.

Chapter One

Reaching through the dense leaves, Alberto grasped the lemon and twisted it off its stalk. The hefty fruit was as large as his hand, and he inspected its waxy pores before lifting it to his nose and sniffing. Nodding, he placed it in the rope bag alongside the muscat grapes. He knew the boy loved to peel the tough grape skins and suck on the sweet pulp inside.

Before he left for the day, he looked down across the stone terraces of his land. Below the lemon trees ran lines of aged almond trees, their branches heavy with nuts. Further down, rows of gnarled grape vines stood stoutly in the dusty ground.

At the bottom, softly shaded by pine trees, lay Alberto's garden, where herbs and flowers flourished. This small patch took more work than all the rest, and carrying the water from the stone irrigation channel tired him. But whenever he picked a large bunch of scented flowers to leave at his wife's grave, he knew his garden would be the last thing he would give up.

When his wife was alive, the two of them would walk to their land together. Over the three kilometres he would listen to her good-humoured chatter about the children and the foreigners whose villas she cleaned. These days, however, Alberto's joints ached at the change of the seasons, and often his own weariness surprised him. He had been reluctantly grateful when one of his daughters and her husband had presented him with a second-hand moped a few years ago. 'Apu's put-put' the boy called it, and Alberto used it regularly to come to the land, and on the odd occasion when he had to go to town.

Now, the old man carefully strapped the bag onto the back of the moped, kicked away the stand with the heel of his espadrille and climbed on. Pedalling briefly to start the rat-a-tat engine, he steered slowly out onto the main road.

Put-putting home in the late sun, Alberto planned how his grandson could help him pick lemons and harvest the almonds. Together, they would visit the local cafes and restaurants on the beachfront to sell their wares. He told his daughter the boy was an extra pair of hands to help him during the school holidays, but they both knew it was more than that.

When he got back to the village, he parked the bike down the alley beside his apartment, locking it behind an iron grille. Carrying the rope bag, he climbed the tiled stairs to his front door but was surprised to find it open. He wasn't expecting the boy until the weekend.

Inside the cool, shadowy room, his rheumy eyes took a moment to adjust. His daughter was sitting at the table, tugging at a white handkerchief in her hand. Her son stood at her side, stock-still, staring intently with large brown eyes at his grandfather.

Alberto smiled reassuringly at the boy, who seemed to relax a tiny amount.

The old man's voice was gravelly, but his words were soft. 'Rosa? What's wrong?'

His daughter glanced at him briefly. 'There's been an accident.'

Alberto sat opposite her, the raffia seat creaking under his weight. 'Juan Carlos?'

At the mention of her husband's name, his daughter nodded and began to cry, raising the handkerchief to her face to hide her tears. The child looked at his mother anxiously. Alberto wished his wife were here. She had always known the words to use to ease an emotional situation, how to express sympathy with just the touch of her hand. These small gestures of love and support were a mystery to Alberto, so he waited for his daughter to compose herself.

She wiped her eyes and nose with the handkerchief. 'He's been hurt in an explosion,' she explained. 'A boiler at Señor Medina's house. No one knows what happened. Juan Carlos is always so good with the old plumbing.'

Alberto nodded, waiting for his daughter to continue. The boy stood so still and silent the old man had almost forgotten he was there.

Rosa took a deep breath and said, 'He's in the hospital. He has very bad burns. He's stable at the moment, but it's serious. They will know more in the morning.'

'Juan Carlos is a strong man,' said Alberto as kindly as his gruff voice would allow.

His daughter looked at him and sighed. 'You're right, Papá. But I have to be with him tonight. Juan Carlos's mother is at the hospital now and I need to return — but it's no place for a child.'

Alberto looked at his grandson and smiled at him. The boy stared back. 'Of course he can stay here.'

'I didn't have the chance to pack a bag; you could go round to our apartment—'

Alberto shook his head. 'No need. He'll be fine. Now, go to your husband.'

Rosa looked at her father and smiled weakly. 'Thank you.'

Alberto stood and put a large, leathery hand on his grandson's small shoulder. The boy looked up at him.

Rosa stood too and turned to hug her son. Alberto watched the child collapse into his mother's arms, sinking his face into her dark curls. She held him for a few moments before straightening up. Blinking away the tears, she stroked the boy's soft brown hair and smiled brightly at him. 'Now, Tino, be a good boy for Apu. And don't worry about your papá — Grandma and I will be with him tonight.'

She turned to her father and gingerly kissed his bristly cheek. 'Thank you, Papá,' she whispered.

As she left the apartment, closing the door behind her, the old man saw the boy stiffen. Quickly he picked up the rope bag, took Tino's hand and led him into the kitchen. He pulled the fruit out of the bag and put the grapes into the sink. Instinctively, the child leant over to turn on the tap and began washing the dust off the grapes.

Alberto took out the bread he'd bought in the village that morning. He tore the end off the long loaf, then reached up into the cupboard overhead and brought out a small bar of chocolate. Breaking off a few squares, he pushed them deep into the middle of the bread. He turned on the grill of his ancient oven, opened the door and put the bread on the shelf.

The boy had finished washing the grapes, so Alberto passed him a tea towel to dry them while he boiled the kettle. When he'd finished, Tino fetched the bowl from the table in the next room and carefully placed the bunches of grapes in it.

Alberto made the boy a cup of weak tea with milk and sugar, and himself a strong cup of black coffee. The child took great care in carrying the glass bowl full of fruit to the table, then sat on a chair while his grandfather placed his tea in front of him. Alberto felt two large brown eyes follow him as he returned to the oven and lifted out the bread.

Insensitive to the heat, he wrapped the toasted loaf in a paper serviette, brought it to the child and sat down opposite him. Tino held it, looking at it as if trying to decide if he was hungry. But as the thin smell of warm, melted chocolate rose from the toasted bread, he began nibbling its crunchy edge.

Alberto sipped his coffee, watching his grandson blowing at and biting past the crust into the chocolate-coated dough. Alberto remembered eating this once as a child and being comforted by the simple treat.

As the boy munched on, Alberto got up and crossed the tiny apartment to the bathroom, which lay off a corridor. He turned the bath taps on full, and while rusty brown water gushed into the bath, he opened the bathroom cabinet. It was almost bare, housing only his razor and shaving foam; toothbrush and paste; a plastic bottle of aspirin that his daughter insisted he take, though he rarely did; and some bubble bath he kept for the boy's visits.

The water had begun to run clear, so he put in the plug and poured out some bubble bath. Then he returned to the boy, who had finished his bread and was holding his mug of tea with both hands.

Alberto placed a hand on the child's head and gently stroked the soft hair.

Tino twisted his head to look up at his grandfather.

'Are you all right?' asked Alberto huskily.

'Yes, Apu,' he nodded, attempting a smile.

'Good. Now finish your tea. It's time for your bath.'

Clean and sleepy, the boy climbed into bed dressed in his grandfather's stripy pyjama top with the sleeves rolled up. Sitting on the bed, the old man tucked the sheet in and laid a light blanket over him.

'Apu?' whispered the little boy.

'Yes.'

'Is Papá going to die?'

'I don't know,' he replied after a brief pause. While he knew his daughter often sugar-coated difficult news, he had always been completely honest with his own children.

The child's large eyes peered up at him.

'I am not a doctor. The hospital is full of doctors. They will do everything they can to make him better.'

'But will he be all right?' Tino persisted.

'Your father is a good man. And he still has a great many things to do in his life. Like watching you grow up. I know he will fight as hard as he can,' said Alberto.

The boy nodded thoughtfully.

'Apu?'

'Yes.'

'How old were you when your papá died?'

The question took him aback, and for a moment he studied his grandchild, considering his answer.

'I don't know,' he said finally, shaking his head.

'Why not?'

'Well,' began Alberto, 'it was the civil war—'

'Spain was in a war? Who were they fighting?'

'Themselves,' said the old man.

'How can a country fight itself?'

'When people have different views, it can end in a fight. You must have seen that at school.'

Tino nodded.

'Some people take the side of one person in the fight, and some people take the other person's side.'

The boy nodded again.

'Well, in this case, the whole country took one side or another. And the whole country fought each other.'

'Who was on the right side?'

'It wasn't that simple. It was a fight between the rich and the poor. Between people who believed in God and people who didn't. Between people who wanted to do things in the traditional way and those who wanted to be more modern.'

'I would be on the side of the poor people who believed in God,' the child stated.

'Well then, you would have been on both sides,' said the old man.

'What?'

'It's true. In those days, the Church was very rich and powerful. The poor workers and farmers wanted change; they wanted their own land and better working conditions. The Church did not want change. So the two were on opposite sides in the war.'

Tino shook his head, unable to understand.

'At the time, I think it seemed an easy decision. You were either for freedom — freedom from poverty, freedom from greedy bosses, even freedom from the Church

— or you wanted things to stay the same, and for the government to be very strict about keeping it that way.'

'And what happened? Who won?'

'The people who wanted to keep things as they were. A man called General Franco won the war.'

'Does he still run Spain?'

'No,' said Alberto. 'Franco died many years ago and Spain has changed a great deal since then.'

'Apu?' said the boy.

'Yes.'

'Which side were you on?'

'I was just a boy. I wasn't on a side.'

'But you must have wanted one side to win more than the other.'

'Well,' said Alberto thoughtfully, 'I lived in an orphanage that was run by the Church, so they taught me that we must believe in God and anyone who didn't was an evil person. But when the war was over, I worked with farmers and workers who had fought on the other side. I knew what it was to be hungry, and can understand why they fought for a better life.'

'But, Apu, you can't be on both sides.'

The old man sighed. 'I do not like violence, but I suppose if I'd had to fight for one side, it would have been the *Rojos*.'

'The *Rojos*? Which side was that?'

'The Republican side. The ones who wanted change.'

'Why the *Rojos*, Apu? Why choose that side?'

9

'It's just a feeling that it was the right side. When it comes to difficult decisions, you can listen to your head or your heart. I am not an educated man, so I listen to my heart.'

The old man smiled at the boy and kissed the top of his head.

'Now,' he said, 'time for sleep.'

'But, Apu, you didn't tell me about your papá.'

'There's nothing to tell. He probably died in the war. Many people did.'

'Probably?'

'I don't remember.'

'You don't remember when your papá went to heaven?' said the boy.

'I was brought up in an orphanage, but I don't remember anything before I arrived there. It's as if my memory was wiped clean. I've tried to remember, but I can't. Not a face, not a name. I tried to find out, but many records were destroyed during the war.'

'How old were you when you went to live at the orphanage?'

'About your age, maybe? I don't know.'

'I don't understand,' said the boy. He shook his head in puzzlement.

'I know which year I arrived at the orphanage. But I don't know what year I was born.'

Tino thought for a moment, his brow wrinkled. 'So,' he said hesitantly, 'so you don't know how old you are? Even now?'

'No.'
'And you don't know when your birthday is?'
'No,' said Alberto. 'I don't have a birthday.'

Chapter Two

ISABEL

Afternoon, 7 March 1937

I look at the pitiful box of vegetables and my stomach sinks. How am I going to feed nearly a hundred orphans on such a meagre amount?

'Jorge!' I shout through the open kitchen window.

'Señorita?' comes the reply as Jorge's face appears outside.

'Are there any more vegetables in the garden? Look at this delivery we've just received – I can't feed them all on this.'

'There's not much, señorita, but I'll see what I can do.'

'Thank you, Jorge,' I smile. At least I know I can trust someone to help.

Rummaging around in the pantry, I find some old potatoes. With the eggs, I can make some dumplings. Thank the good Lord for our chickens.

Before she died, my mother had taught me how to make a meal from barely nothing. As the oldest child, it was a skill that helped me feed my father and five siblings. When my sister turned fifteen, I taught her all I could about running the home so that I could leave — our father needed one less mouth to feed.

My sister and I had been in the market one day when I'd overheard two women talking.

'Did you know they've turned the old house on the hill into an orphanage?' one had said to the other.

'Yes,' the second had replied. 'I heard they were bringing children from both sides.'

'Republican children too?'

'That's right. They want to teach them the mistakes of their parents. And the priests will make them accept God into their lives.'

'Well, that's something, isn't it? At least there will be a chance of salvation for the children. Can you imagine? Those poor things having no Communion, growing up without faith? I think it's disgusting. What kind of parent—'

I had interrupted the women to ask if they thought the orphanage would be taking on staff, and they told me where I could go to find out.

I'd been hired by Señora Peña, a large, red-faced woman whose husband was an administrator for the Nationalists. The orphanage had already taken in children from all around the region and she needed a cook to run the kitchen.

As the war has gone on, I've noticed more children

arrive, and the food boxes become smaller. Every meal-time is a challenge, but I do my best to see these children have as good a meal as I can serve them.

As I set to preparing the dinner, the señora waddles into the kitchen and places a large silver tray on the table.

'The bishop has finished taking coffee with the father and is doing a tour of the classes. He wishes to visit the dining room when the children are eating their dinner, so make sure the meal is on time and plentiful.'

'Yes, señora,' I reply. There is little point in showing her the half-empty box of vegetables; she would only say there was more than enough for such small stomachs.

'And tidy this mess up in case he wishes to see the kitchen.' She waves her plump hand over the tray before bustling out of the room.

I finish making the dumplings and prepare a stew with the vegetables from the box. Jorge arrives with a handful of carrots, which I gratefully accept and add to the stew.

'Jorge, you deserve a cup of coffee,' I say, picking up the coffee pot.

'There's coffee?' asks Jorge, surprised.

'The bishop is here,' I reply.

'Ah,' says Jorge, nodding as he sits at the long kitchen table.

While the stew and dumplings bubble and the coffee

brews, I clear the best china from the tray. As I pick up the plates, a glint of colour catches my eye. There, nestling under a saucer, is a piece of paper I recognize immediately. It is a chocolate-bar wrapper.

Holding my breath, I gently pull the paper, praying it isn't empty. It isn't. Unnoticed, the last few squares of chocolate have been left, hidden and forgotten.

'Look, Jorge,' I whisper, holding up the chocolate.

Jorge's eyes widen. 'What are you going to do with that?' he asks.

I know he is hoping I will share it with him. And for a moment I am tempted. I can't remember the last time I tasted chocolate — probably not since before the war began.

'I'll know when the time is right,' I say. I fold the wrapper carefully round the precious squares and pop it into my apron pocket.

Jorge tries to hide his disappointment as he nods his consent. 'I'll go and set up the chairs for dinner,' he says quietly as he limps out.

Poor Jorge. He told me he was injured in a farming accident as a young boy. He says his limp has never bothered him, but I know it does. He rarely talks about it, but others do, and I know it was his leg that stopped him from fighting for the Nationalist forces. Now he feels he's failed to do his duty.

I know this because every Sunday, Señora Peña allows me to have the morning off to go to church. After the service, sitting in the shade of an old tree, the women sit and gossip. One day, I asked them about my friend at the orphanage and the story came out.

Jorge had a younger brother. An idealistic young man, he had become a local member of the Socialist Party. He had driven Jorge demented with his talk of oppression and rights for workers. Jorge is a religious man, and when his brother had spoken of a godless society, Jorge had not been able to hold his tongue. Their bitter argument turned violent and Jorge had thrown his brother out of the house.

The young man left for the city and became a political activist. Two years ago, Jorge heard that his brother had been arrested. The family have not heard from him since. Jorge still does not know if his brother was executed while a political prisoner, or if he was released when the Coalition of Socialists won the elections last year. Either way, Jorge believes the Republican movement took his brother from him.

When the war began, Jorge tried to join the army to fight for the Nationalists. I think he saw it as his chance to exert revenge on the Republicans – to beat the *Rojos*. He was rejected because of his limp. He tried again in two different towns but was told the pride of the Spanish National Army would not allow it. He argued that his passion for the cause would make him a better soldier than if he had two good legs. He was still refused.

Looking for another way to serve the Nationalists, he found work at the orphanage. He provides as much food as he can from the grounds and helps out as a handyman. I know he smuggles a few of the vegetables home to his wife and children, but he is a good man and cares for the orphans.

And the good Lord knows the poor little things need someone to care for them. They range in age from toddlers barely able to feed themselves to young adults who will soon be sent back out into the world. Many have been taken from their parents; some have seen their parents shot; all have witnessed things a child should not see.

The Church directs a strict programme of re-education at the orphanage, which the priests and Señora Peña follow enthusiastically. So the children are taught, often cruelly, that their parents were evil *Rojos* whose actions have condemned them to an eternity in hell. The father drills the children until their *generalísimo* salute is perfect.

Jorge and I are not allowed to spend time with the orphans. We keep our heads down and provide what we can from the garden and the meagre rations the Church sends. It is our small contribution to the war.

But despite knowing the fight against the anti-religious Republicans is right and just, my heart hurts when I see the little ones. They are constantly hungry, their shoes are worn through, and despite our best efforts, they are crawling with lice. And while the grand old house should be filled with their laughter and play, it is often silent with fear. These children have learnt to accept their lot. While the country fights on, their war is already lost.

As some of the older children and I finish serving the measly stew to the orphans, the bishop arrives at the dining room, flanked by the father and Señora Peña. Quickly, I withdraw to the kitchen and start the washing-up.

Jorge's face appears at the window. 'Isabel, another one's just arrived.'

Nodding, I dry my hands on my apron and hurry through the back door. The last thing Señora Peña will want is a scruffy orphan arriving unannounced in the middle of the bishop's visit.

Outside, a truck is parked on the driveway. Jorge is talking to the driver, a tall soldier, smart in his uniform. Beside them is a small boy. He is covered in dust and dirt, his shorts and jacket are torn, and one knee is caked in dried blood. He stands, looking at his boots.

'Good afternoon, señorita,' says the soldier as I approach.

'Good afternoon,' I smile at him. The soldier's eyes are implausibly dark and the sunlight makes them twinkle. He smiles back – so warmly and generously that I stop, realizing how rare such a smile is these days.

'Who is this?' I ask, nodding at the boy.

The soldier ruffles the boy's hair and says, 'My

friend here doesn't talk much. He didn't seem keen on telling me his name. Or anything else for that matter. But he needs a new home. This is the only orphanage I could think of, so I brought him here.'

Bending down, I look at the boy. Sun-bleached curls frame his face.

'Hello,' I say cheerfully. 'My name is Isabel. What's yours?'

The boy doesn't even seem to register my existence and continues to look at his boots.

I try again. 'Where are you from, child?'

He continues to ignore me.

After a pause, Jorge asks the soldier where he found the boy.

The soldier glances around, but realizing there's no one to hear, he says quietly, 'I heard the fighting had reached my home town. I was delivering supplies not far away, so I took a detour to check my family were all right. Father Francisco from my family's church was looking after him. He wouldn't tell me how the child had come to him, but he asked that I take him out of danger.'

The soldier looks down at the boy sadly. 'He hasn't spoken a word, and we've been driving most of the day.'

'He's probably seen things he doesn't want to talk about,' says Jorge softly.

'We passed a stretch where there had recently been a battle. There were dead *Rojos* near the road. It seemed to affect him quite badly,' agrees the soldier.

As I reach to stroke the boy's face, he flinches and, in

his terror, looks at me for an instant. His eyes are soft brown, flecked with green. I hear a rustle from his pocket and notice a piece of paper flutter to the ground.

Picking it up, I see it is the torn triangle of an envelope. On one side, the name ALBERT ROMERO is clearly written. There is more writing on the other side. This is a little harder to decipher, but with a gasp I realize that it is an address in England.

Quickly, I squirrel it into the pocket of my apron and look up. The soldier is sharing a cigarette with Jorge and chatting about whether the fighting will reach us. I don't think they've seen the piece of paper.

Grasping the boy's hand, I say loudly, 'Jorge, I'm taking the boy into the kitchen to get him cleaned up. Don't be long – the señora may need you.'

I turn to the soldier. 'Thank you, señor.'

The soldier smiles back as I turn and walk away.

The boy trots along obediently beside me. As I open the back door, I turn and see the soldier is still looking at me. I lift my hand in a small wave before shooing the child inside.

In the kitchen, I motion the boy over to the long oak table, where he sits, still looking at his boots. I open the bread bin and take out the last crust. I was saving it for my supper, but I can do without. With my finger I drill a hole into the middle of the hard bread and then reach into my apron pocket and take out the chocolate. Unwrapping it carefully, I stuff the chocolate into the bread and pop it into the warm oven.

Then I rinse a cloth in water and approach the boy, who eyes me suspiciously.

'I'm just going to wash your face, Alberto,' I say gently.

I lift his chin and start to wipe the grime off his face. He looks around slowly, taking in his new surroundings.

'This is an orphanage, Alberto. There are lots of other boys and girls like you here. You'll soon have friends. How old are you, Alberto? Have you been to school? You will have lessons here. The priests take the classes and will teach you to read and write.'

I continue cleaning the boy and speaking gently to him as I do so, although he does not respond. Eventually, his face and hands are clean and I rinse the filthy cloth in the sink. Then, opening the oven, I take out the toasted bread, wrap it in a little paper and hand it to the boy.

He accepts it sceptically and sits, holding it.

'Alberto,' I say quietly, hunching down to his level. 'Alberto, the orphanage is run by people who do not like the *Rojos*.' I reach into my pocket, bring out the piece of paper and hold it in front of him. 'Who gave you this?' I ask.

The boy looks at me intently but remains silent.

'Alberto, this is an address in England. Did you meet a Republican soldier? Did he give you this?'

The boy just looks at me.

I sigh and brush a dusty curl off his face.

'Alberto,' I say seriously, holding the paper in front

of his face, 'this orphanage is run by the Church and supported by the Nationalists. When you do decide to talk again, do not speak of this.'

I stand, open the oven door and throw in the paper. It instantly curls and blackens; then a small orange flame flares, eating the paper until just a grey sliver of dust is left to settle on the floor of the stove.

I shut the door and turn back to the boy, but he is not looking. He has taken a bite out of the chocolate-soaked bread and is chewing it slowly.

He looks up at me, and I think I see the tiniest trace of a smile.

Chapter Three

Alberto held the little boy's hand tightly as they walked along the corridor. The smell of disinfectant was pervasive and the child wrinkled his nose. Towards the end of the walkway, they reached a long window and Alberto slowed, looking in.

A large metal bed stood in the middle of the room. Lying on top of the white sheets, bound in white bandages, lay a motionless figure. Wires and tubes appeared from under the wrappings and were connected to a machine beside the bed. A woman in blue pyjamas, cap and face mask was adjusting a drip.

Sitting in a chair beside the bed was Juan Carlos's mother. A semi-transparent yellow garment covered her customary black dress, and plastic booties concealed her black slippers. She too wore a blue face mask and cap. Her eyes were shut and Alberto couldn't tell if she was deep in prayer or dozing.

Leaning over the bandaged head, talking gently to the man within was his daughter. She was wearing the same clinical garments as her mother-in-law, her long, dark curls swept up into a cap.

Absorbed in watching his daughter, he didn't notice Tino let go of his hand, stand on his tiptoes and peer into the room – not until he heard a small gasp. Looking down, he saw the boy's mouth open in shock and his wide eyes filling with tears. Juan Carlos's mother's head snapped up in time to see the old man pulling the reluctant child away from the window.

Leading him to some nearby chairs, Alberto helped the boy into the seat and sat next to him.

'Apu, was that really Papá?' he whispered. Large tears ran down his cheeks.

'Yes, it was,' he replied gently.

At that moment, the door opened and Tino's mother walked out of the room. He jumped up and ran to her, and she took off her mask and bent down to hug him.

Alberto stood. After some quiet words, his daughter wiped the tears from her son's eyes and led him back to Alberto.

'Well?' he asked.

Rosa sighed. He could see she was exhausted.

'The doctor was worried Juan Carlos would go into shock last night. But he's done well over the past few hours and they say he is stable now. The pain relief is very strong. He's not conscious, but we speak to him constantly, so he knows he's not alone.'

Alberto nodded.

'I've been talking to the nurses. They say over the next few days it is essential that he avoids any risk of infection.' She stopped speaking and looked down at her son, who held her hand with both of his. 'I cannot leave Juan Carlos. Could Tino stay with you a little longer?'

'You know he can stay as long as is necessary.'

Smiling weakly, Rosa nodded gratefully to her father.

Tap, tap, tap — the long stick struck the top branches and a hard brown shower of nuts bounced onto the green netting under the tree. Tino waited until the last almond had fallen, then, picking out the occasional leaf, gathered the nuts and put them into a large plastic bucket. Then he stepped back to the edge of the netting as his grandfather moved over to some other almond-laden branches and began tapping again.

When the tub was full, Alberto carefully put down the stick. Nodding to the boy, he picked up the tub and carried it over to the edge of the terrace, where they sat, in the shade of a lemon tree. The sun was still in full heat, and the pale brown earth on the terrace was cracked like an over-baked cake.

Alberto opened a bottle of water he had brought and handed it to the boy, who took a long drink. The old man took a few gulps and settled the bottle in the shade. Then he and Tino set to peeling the hard, leathery husks from their harvest, throwing the skins on the ground and putting the nuts with their distinctive pitted shells into a canvas bag.

'Apu?' asked the boy as they worked.

'Yes.'

'If you don't know when your birthday is, do you still get birthday presents or have a party?'

'No.'

'But just because you don't remember the date doesn't mean you can't just pick another date.'

'Hmmmm.'

'It's my birthday soon. I'm going to be eight.'

'I know.'

'Apu?'

'Yes.'

'Would you like to share my birthday with me? We could have a party together.'

The old man stopped and looked at the boy. 'That's very kind of you,' he said.

He remembered the years that his wife had tried to do the same thing. Although the government had given him a date for his papers – 1 January – he had never thought of it as his birthday. Instead, María Luisa had suggested dates, both random and those that were important to them. He had never agreed, saying it was silly and pointless. But when their children had come along, he had enjoyed the presents and parties she'd organized for them, glad when they'd taken it for granted. That was how a childhood should be.

'I'm too old for birthday parties now,' he said, smiling.

'But, Apu,' continued Tino, 'everyone should have a

birthday. Even Grandma has a birthday every year —
that's how we know she's so old.'

'Do I need a birthday to know that I am old?' asked
Alberto.

'No,' agreed the boy. 'But don't you want to have a
birthday?'

The old man shrugged. 'I have managed all these
years without one.'

'Everyone should have a birthday, Apu.'

'Why is that?'

'Because a birthday is your day. It's the day when
everybody comes to visit you. They bring gifts, and food,
and you are with the people who love you. It's a special
day, Apu.'

Alberto looked at the boy, bemused.

'You don't know, Apu. Because you've never had a
birthday. You don't know how it feels. It's a good day.
I want you to know how it feels.'

Alberto nodded. 'Well, maybe you're right. But I
would need a date for a birthday.'

'You can share mine.'

'No.' The old man shook his head. 'That is your
special day, not mine. It's good of you to offer to share
it, but that day is just for you.'

Tino frowned, peeling the tough coat off an almond.
'Then we will have to find your birthday,' he said.

That evening, Alberto sat in his weathered armchair,
sipping a glass of brandy. His other daughter, Cristina,

had married well and she and her husband lived in Madrid. Each year at Three Kings, they would visit with their family. They would present Alberto with an expensive bottle of brandy, which he accepted uncomfortably and savoured in private.

The television shouted the results of the lottery, but Alberto paid it no attention. The conversation about his birthday tap, tap, tapped at his mind. It had unsettled him, and he could not understand why. He had spent so many years not knowing his birthday. Why should the idea of it start to nag at him now? Was it that he was getting old, that he wanted to know before he died?

Suddenly, a shriek came from the other room.

Running next door and switching on the bedroom light, he saw the boy sitting up in bed, glossy with sweat. They had been to Rosa's apartment earlier and picked up a bag of clothes, so the child was dressed in his own pyjamas. A small, tatty brown bear lay discarded beside him on the bed.

Alberto moved the bear so he could sit down and gathered the boy into his arms, stroking his damp head.

'Was it a dream?' he asked gruffly.

The boy started sobbing, clinging tightly to his grandfather.

Alberto hushed the boy, rocking him gently.

'Tell me,' he urged in a whisper.

Hiccupping air, the boy burrowed his head deeper into his grandfather's chest. 'It was Papá. He was trying to get out of the bandages, but they just kept wrapping more and more round him. I was shouting to let him out, but they didn't hear me. Apu, they wouldn't listen to me.'

'Shhh,' said the old man. He held the child tightly and rocked him. He tried to reassure him with words he believed to be true. 'The doctors and nurses are helping him get better. They're looking after your papá. Soon they'll take the bandages off and you'll see him again.'

Reluctantly, the old man remembered in the years after the war seeing men horribly disfigured by burns. But, these days, the medics could do so much more for the victims. At least, he hoped they could. He felt the child's tears soak into his shirt.

'Now, now, little one. It was just a bad dream. Dreams like that don't come true. Forget about it and think of things that make you happy. Think how when your papá is better, you'll play football with him at the park.'

Tino snuffled noisily.

'Think about your birthday party,' whispered the old man. 'Your cake, covered with cream, and all those presents waiting to be opened. And the party with your friends and the games you'll play.'

'And your party too, Apu,' sniffed the boy sleepily. 'When we find your birthday.'

Alberto smiled, relieved that something had distracted the child from his distress.

'Yes,' said Alberto quietly. 'We'll have a party when we find my birthday.'

He felt the exhausted child relax in his arms and laid him down on the pillow, tucking the bear into the crook of his arm. Then he stayed awhile, making sure the boy was sound asleep, before going back into the living room, leaving the door open.

Sighing, he rubbed his eyes, picked up the glass of brandy and swallowed the remainder, relishing the sensation as the liquid slid down his throat.

Over the next few days, Alberto and the boy spent all of their time together. The old man was concerned to see Tino subdued and tense, so spent as much time as possible on his land keeping the child busy.

Together, they visited tree after tree, tapping the almonds to the ground. When all the nuts were harvested and rid of their husks, the old man loaded the last canvas bags onto the moped and walked the heavy bike along the road.

Back at the apartment, Alberto took two chairs downstairs to the street outside his apartment. He and Tino sat on the pavement, the bags of nuts between them. The old man gave the boy a simple nutcracker.

'Mind your fingers,' he told him.

While the boy set to cracking his first nut, Alberto stood a tall log between his legs and took a small hammer out of his pocket. Lifting an almond out of the nearest canvas bag, he placed it on the top of the neatly cut log and brought the hammer down on it with a swift rap. The almond shell split neatly, and he swept the broken bits onto the ground as he dropped the wrinkled nut into a large glass jar next to the boy.

'Apu?' said Tino as he emptied broken shells onto the pavement.

'Yes.'

'Where was the orphanage you lived at?'

'Inland. It was a big hacienda surrounded by farm-land. In the summer, it was as hot as here, but in the winter, it was bitterly cold and often snowed.'

'But, Apu, now you live by the sea. Why did you come here?'

'When the war ended, we were moved to a bigger institution in the city. That was a terrible place and I left as soon as I could. But the country was very poor then and there were no jobs. I was young, but I went looking for work and took it where I could find it. At harvest times, I would work on the farms for my food and keep. At other times, I would work in towns to help the builders reconstruct everything that had been destroyed in the war.

'I travelled all over the country, sometimes walking, sometimes catching a lift on the back of a cart. After a while, I came to the coast. I found work at a farm during the olive harvest. It was at that farm I met my wife, your grandmother.'

Alberto remembered the farm and the long, sunny days he'd spent plucking the fat black olives from the trees, chatting easily with the farmer's youngest daugh-ter. She'd had curvy hips, a sassy attitude and a raucous laugh. She'd made him smile, and at lunch when the family and workers had sat at a long trestle table to eat, she'd served him larger portions than anyone else.

Her father had joked that if María Luisa continued to feed him so well, Alberto would become too fat to work and they'd have to let him go. Alberto had blushed, not used to being included in the lively banter of close family and friends. But the family had warmed to the shy boy María Luisa adored, and when the olive harvest had finished, her father had found more work for him on the farm.

'And so you wanted to stay?' asked his grandson.

'And so I wanted to stay.'

'And you never went back to where the orphanage was?'

'No.'

'We should go there.'

'Why?'

'Because that's where we should start looking for your birthday.'

'Why do you think I'll find my birthday there?'

'I don't know. But I think it's the only place to start, Apu. Don't you?'

Alberto smiled and nodded at the boy.

'Well, if I were going to go looking for my birthday, you're right — it's the best place to start,' he said.

Looking up from his nutcracker, the boy smiled at his grandfather. It was only a small smile, but Alberto was relieved to see it.

'Well, you two look very pleased with yourselves,' said a cheery voice.

A wide woman walked up the street towards them. She was dressed in a blue-and-white patterned dress and carpet slippers. Her rosy cheeks glowed, and her broad smile revealed a missing tooth. Her grey hair was set in large curls, the rollers only recently removed.

'Señora Ortiz,' said Alberto. He politely nodded his head and set down the hammer.

'We're going looking for Apu's birthday, señora,' said Tino gleefully.

'Are you? Well, I hope I can come to the party when you find it!' said the señora. She winked at Alberto.

'Oh yes, Apu. We'll have to organize your first ever birthday party! Mamá can make all the food and there will be presents.'

'That's a lovely idea, little one,' said the señora. She reached down and pinched Tino's cheek. 'The whole village will come to Alberto's birthday party.'

Alberto smiled and shook his head at the silliness.

'But, Papá, I don't understand,' said Rosa, frowning.

'It's just for a few days. I think it will be good for him.'

The old man had thought long and hard about it. Each evening, they had come to the hospital to look through the window at Juan Carlos, and each night, the nightmares had returned. Despite spending a busy day outdoors in the sunshine, the child had grey shadows under his eyes.

Worried about him, Alberto had let his grandson chatter on about the search for his birthday, happy that it distracted him from the anxiety he felt over his father. Finally, a week after Juan Carlos's accident, he'd decided to ask his daughter if he could take his grandson away. They would travel inland to the orphanage – if it was still there. Most likely, that would be the end of the search, but at least the journey and change of scene would take Tino's mind off his father.

'But a family should be together – especially at a time like this,' said his daughter. 'And what about Tino? Shouldn't he be near his father?'

'He's having nightmares, Rosa. Seeing his father like this upsets him. He doesn't want to say anything to you, but he's afraid to come into the hospital.'

His daughter looked at him, still confused. 'But what about me, Papá? Doesn't he want to be with me?'

The old man looked at his daughter and saw the anxiety in her eyes. Perhaps he shouldn't have suggested it. A nurse had taken Tino off to the canteen to get a drink and Alberto had seen his opportunity to talk privately to Rosa. But it seemed he had made a mistake. The last thing he wanted to do was upset her more. His daughter knew what was best for her son, not him – it should be her decision.

'Let him go,' said Juan Carlos's mother from across the corridor.

Alberto and his daughter both looked round in surprise. They hadn't realized she had heard their conversation.

'But—' said Rosa.

'No. It's not good for him to see his father like this. He enjoys being with his grandfather. And a trip will be good for both of them.'

'We'll only be away a few days,' said Alberto gently. 'And Cristina arrives tomorrow afternoon. You'll have your sister with you.'

'Well . . .' said his daughter.

'By the time they come home, his father will be much better,' said Juan Carlos's mother firmly.

'Ask him, Rosa,' said Alberto. 'Ask the boy what he wants to do.' As his daughter looked up at him, Alberto nodded to her. After what seemed like an age, she slowly nodded back at him.

Alberto looked across at Juan Carlos's mother as she prepared to go back into the hospital room, tying her mask behind the back of her head. He smiled his thanks at her.

'But,' said Rosa, 'where did you say you were going?'

'He wants to find my birthday.'

'And, after all these years, you want to look for it?'

'Rosa, it's caught his imagination. It's all he talks about. And I let him, because while he's thinking about my birthday, he's not thinking about his father in hospital.'

'But what about you, Papá? Do you want to go back?'

'It was sixty-five years ago; we won't find anything. I expect nothing.'

But in truth, he was looking forward to the trip. As a young man, he had spent years on the road, never knowing where the next day would take him. Meeting people and seeing new places had given him an education, and sometimes he wished he'd travelled further to see what the world had to offer. But marrying and settling down had been good for him, and he had cherished the security he had found with his small family.

The thought of the trip filled him with a sense of anticipation he hadn't experienced in many years.

'Well, if you do find your birthday, I hope you're not expecting presents for all those years we missed!'

Alberto smiled warmly — it was the first time since Juan Carlos's accident that he had seen his daughter's face relax and her eyes soften. If Tino was happy to go, perhaps this trip would be good for all of them.

Chapter Four

Smoothing down my hair, I place my hat carefully on my head. Then I run my thumb and forefinger down my moustache, checking every hair is in place. Next I feel my collar, to make sure there are no creases. And lastly, adjusting my gun holster, I look down and inspect my gleaming jackboots for dust.

A man gains respect by maintaining excellence in everything he does. It is important my men look up to me, not just for my intelligence and courage, but also for my pride in the uniform and all that it stands for.

Perhaps it is because I have been in uniform most of my life that I hold the greatest of regard for it. Born into a military family, there was never any question that I would be anything other than an officer. My sisters are married to soldiers of high rank, and their sons will be enrolled into military academies at a young age, as I was. Like me, they will realize the honour of their duty. They will learn that the military is the guardian of Spain.

Satisfied, I step outside the small house my squadron has commandeered. The village is quiet for the time of morning. A few of my men stroll around the square; they are far too relaxed for my liking. We have been informed the Republican rabble is nearby and we must be ever vigilant.

Two young women scuttle past, their dark shawls pulled around their faces. They avoid looking at me — they are, no doubt, *Rojos*.

I bark at my men, and startled, they turn and salute me. Instantly their backs straighten and they look like professional soldiers. I command them to patrol the outskirts of the village and report back to me in an hour.

I fully intend to be a general before too long. While my family connections stand me in good stead for promotion, I want to prove my merit to my superiors. My whole life has been designed to take me to the highest levels of the army, and this war has propelled me at even greater speed towards this goal. I will become a general and help Franco achieve a glorious victory.

Scanning the square, I decide to visit the church. Usually, there is a decent cup of coffee and helpful information to be garnered when one introduces oneself to the clergy. They like to show their support in any way they can.

The church sits on one side of the square. I push open the heavy wooden door and stride inside. It is cool and dark and smells of dust and old incense. In the gloom, I see a few elderly women, kneeling, praying and worrying rosaries. To one side of the altar, an ancient man with a crooked back sweeps the floor. He glances at me and brushes his way into a shadowed corner and out of sight.

My heels click on the stone floor as I approach the altar. When I reach the front, I stop, drop to one knee, cross myself and close my eyes. At that moment, I hear murmurings nearby. Rising, I walk quietly towards the noise. By a side door is the priest, dressed in his black robes. He is talking in a low voice to a small, filthy boy.

'Good morning, Father,' I say loudly.

The priest jumps at the sound of my voice and turns to me, pushing the child behind him. Probably in his early forties, he is relatively tall with receding hair and silver spectacles. The other priests I have known have generally been portly, but this man is well built for his age. For an instant, I imagine him in an officer's uni-form, and he looks good in it.

'I am Captain García,' I introduce myself. 'My men and I are here to maintain the security of this town.'

The priest nods and smiles stiffly at me. This is not the sort of welcome I am used to from a cleric.

'Good morning, Captain. I am pleased to meet you. My name is Father Francisco. This is my church, and my village.'

I glance around and notice the old women have slipped out and the church is now empty.

'Father Francisco, there are reports of Republicans

in the area, and as you are a respected clergyman of the community, I wish to discuss with you how my men can defend this town. Are you free now?' I nod towards the dirty child.

The priest steps behind the boy, putting his hands on his shoulders protectively.

'Yes, of course. Please accept my apologies. Alberto here has recently arrived at the church. It seems he has lost his family and I am looking after him while we arrange where he will go.'

'I'm sure you can find an orphanage near here,' I reply sharply, annoyed that he puts this child before the welfare of my men and our cause.

A look crosses the priest's face and I wonder momentarily if I have angered him before dismissing the thought.

'Yes, Captain,' he replies politely.

With that, he opens the small door beside him and indicates for me to step outside. The door opens onto a walled cemetery in the church grounds, where stone crosses and gravestones stand to attention in the browned grass. A large carob tree casts a little shade on the rear of the churchyard.

The priest follows me and the boy steps out of the church after him. Pulling the door shut, the priest gestures to a bench leaning against the church wall and the boy obediently sits on it.

I notice the priest look at the ground. I follow his gaze and see I am standing within the rectangular outline of a grave. At its head is a simple cross, but there is no name inscribed on it. It is completely blank.

As I step off the grave and onto the gravel path, the priest asks, 'So, Captain, how may I be of service?'

'Father, I have not breakfasted yet,' I reply. 'I was wondering if we might take a cup of coffee together.'

'Captain,' says the priest smoothly, 'I'm embarrassed to say that I have no coffee. The cafe on the plaza is still open — they serve chicory coffee — perhaps you would like to talk there?'

'Do you not receive extra rations, Father?' I ask, puzzled.

'What I receive, I share,' says the priest piously. 'There are others in more need than myself, and I am more than content with chicory.'

'Never mind the chicory,' I snap. I am becoming annoyed at this confounding behaviour. 'What do you know of the *Rojos*' movements in the area? Will they find support in this village?'

'I'm afraid I have no news to tell of Republicans in this area, Captain,' says the priest, tight-lipped.

'Father, I am sure you are aware of your obligation to tell me of any *Rojo* activity here,' I nudge. I sense his reluctance to divulge information.

Taking a deep breath, the priest speaks quietly. 'Captain, as all over Spain, this village is split. Families, friends and neighbours have been divided by allegiances to one side or the other. The young men have all left to fight. The elderly and women who remain do not voice their loyalties, but fear and distrust lie close to the surface. Just yesterday, we had to pull apart two sisters who would have gouged each other's eyes out if left to fight. Their husbands joined opposing armies, and—'

'This country is at war, Father,' I interrupt. I am not interested in tattle tales of his villagers, and I will not be drawn into a discussion about some women. 'Just tell me what you know about the enemy's movements around here.'

The priest looks at me, his face set. 'There have been rumours that the fighting is drawing near, but I know nothing more. In my services, I continue to pray for a conclusion to the war and a lasting peace for the people of this country.'

'I assume that you are praying for a glorious victory for the *generalísimo*.' I scowl at him. I am growing suspicious of this priest. Could it be that he is a collaborator?

'I do not feel it is my place to take sides. I only know that I am a follower of Christ the Lord,' he replies softly.

As the man talks, I feel a rage stir in me.

'Father,' I say, seething, 'must I remind you, of all people, of the attacks on the Church, and the brutality shown to Catholic priests? The Nationalists stand with the Spanish Church. Together, we will repel this evil.'

'Sir,' replies the priest quietly, 'my position in this village is to support my flock through these difficult times. My only weapon is the word of the Lord. In His glory He tells us to strive for peace, He teaches us that wisdom is better than the weapons of war, and—'

As he speaks, the fury in me rises and I shout at him, 'How dare you preach at me! I have personally seen the bodies of men and women who were buried alive — their only crime being their faith in God. I have seen the ruins of churches where Catholics were locked inside, burnt to death as Republican firefighters looked on. Thousands of your brethren have been murdered and you speak the words of a pacifist! Do their deaths mean nothing to you?'

'Captain,' he replies, his voice low, 'I pray for every soul lost in this futile war. But atrocities should not be matched by further atrocities. Where will it end? Our country will be only flooded with blood.'

'Good God, man!' I holler. 'If it were not for the support of the righteous of this country, your Church would have been destroyed. And where would you be then? As poor as the pathetic creatures scraping a living in the fields.'

The priest pulls his shoulders back and looks me straight in the eye. For a moment, we glare directly at each other. Behind his spectacles, his dark green eyes flash with passion, and as I look into them, I see him make a decision.

'I would be honoured to work alongside the poor,' he says. His voice wavers, but his words are emphatic.

We stare at each other, both aware of what he has done. These are the words of a Republican: he is a traitor.

In that moment, it is my turn to make a decision.

I suck a ball of saliva behind my teeth and spit it at him with all the venom I can muster.

The spit lands on his left cheek, and for an instant, I am as shocked as he is. I know what I have done is a sacrilege, unforgivable. But this is not a man of the Church. He is the enemy.

As he stands, still staring at me, I turn to leave, but suddenly I hear a shrill voice scream, 'No!'

It is the boy. He has been watching everything, and as I look, he runs towards me.

'Alberto, stop!' shouts the priest, but the boy ignores him. As he reaches me, I see his hands are clenched into small fists, and with a speed and strength I did not expect of him, he lands a blow on my thigh.

It hurts more than I let on, but as he lifts his other arm to hit me again, I strike him hard across the face with the back of my hand. The clout sends him crashing to the ground and he skids across the dirt.

I watch the priest dash over to the boy, spittle still hanging from his cheek.

Taking a deep breath, I adjust my jacket and holster, check my hat and run my fingers over my moustache.

'I can see little reason to defend this pitiful place and its inhabitants,' I say with disdain. Looking down at the priest kneeling by the boy, who is nursing a bloodied knee, I conclude with the words, 'It seems the enemy is already here.'

With that, I turn on my heel and stride past them.

The wind is strong and the eucalyptus trees creak high above us. For the last ten minutes, it has been quiet on both sides. The brown dust loosened by gunshots has been whipped up and swirls round the patch of land between us. It makes it hard to see where the enemy hides, and the wind steals the sounds that would give them away.

'Captain?' queries the soldier crouching beside me by the ditch wall. His build is solid and stocky, but his gun shakes in his hand, betraying his fear.

'We wait,' I say quietly to him. 'We'll let them give themselves away.'

I glance along the ditch, checking my men. They all keep their heads below the top of the dusty line of fire, awaiting my command. Glancing over the top of the earthy ridge, I see the fallen men lying between us and the Republican enemy.

Earlier in the day, my men brought me word that a band of *Rojos* had been spotted a few miles out of the village. We assembled quickly and went out on foot. Surprise has been our greatest weapon and I knew we did not have time to wait for the reinforcements and armoured vehicles we had been expecting.

We came up behind them near a stretch of road about five miles from the village. They were ambling along, relaxed and chatting among themselves. They must have had no communications that we were in the area, but that is no excuse. At the very least, they should have been securing their flanks. The lack of military discipline appalled me. I quietly directed my men into a nearby ditch, where they swiftly set up the machine gun. And on my command, they opened fire.

Of course, many of the Republican soldiers were shot in the back, and those that turned towards us had little time to raise their guns before we scythed them down. The few that survived managed to dive behind a small hillock on the other side of a dusty patch of land from us. They started firing and shots flew in both directions. Then the wind sprang up, swirling dust around us all, and the firing ceased. Now both sides are waiting for the other to make the first move.

Two of my men are dead. Or rather, one is dead. The other continues to moan and plead for help where he lies, but I refuse to let my men rescue him. I can see no point in risking more soldiers for the sake of a man who will most likely die anyway. I saw the hate in my men's eyes when I refused to let them collect him, but I don't care: I know they will channel that hatred into fighting the enemy.

The gunner sits nearby, our only machine gun wedged into the rocks beside him. He is young, probably about nineteen, and keeps his short hair neatly cropped. I know his name is Luis, but I would never call him that. I cannot be seen to be too personal with my men.

As I watch the gunner, he digs in his pocket for a packet of cigarettes and lifts one to his mouth with a shaking hand. Then, after more digging, he pulls out a box of matches. The first breaks as he strikes it. The second lights, but his hand is shaking so violently he can't get it close to the cigarette.

Instinctively, I reach out and grip his wrist. Luis looks up at me, surprised, but lets me guide his hand to the cigarette hanging from his lips. As he sucks the life into it, I let go and he nods his thanks.

I can remember when fear had gripped me with such intensity too.

Shortly after the war began, I was given my first command and we were sent to a city that was being occupied. Although my training had been extensive, this was to be my first true battle. However, the *Rojos* had been weakened by the fall of a nearby city, and by the time we arrived, our forces were entering the city's outskirts and we'd joined them.

My instructions had been to take prisoners, but as we stepped over enemy soldiers dead on the road, it was clear that they had been executed. The military academy had instilled in me honour above all, and I did my best to hide my shock.

As we carried on, we heard shots from the city centre. Turning a corner, we came to a small plaza, where dozens of *Rojo* soldiers were standing, their hands behind their heads. They were surrounded by our men, guns trained on them from every direction. A general had noticed me and called me over. Leaving my men, I ran over to speak to him.

After the initial formalities, he said, 'I'm glad you're here, García. I have been instructed to be at the bull-ring. These men need despatching; you may now take over.'

'The prisoners, sir?' I replied, confused.

He looked me square in the face, and I lifted my chin in an attempt to show confidence. I failed.

'This is your first time, isn't it?' he asked quietly.

'Sir, I was highly commended at the academy—'

'Yes, yes, I see,' he interrupted, sighing. 'Look, I know it's not what you learn at the academy, but these filthy *Rojos* need be despatched.'

'But, sir—'

'Just do it!' he snapped. Then, his face softening a little, he said, 'By killing these enemy soldiers, you are protecting your mother and your sisters. Do it in the name of the Lord Himself, for we are the protectorate of the Catholic Church.'

'Yes, sir!' I said loudly, saluting him.

He started towards the motorcycle beside him, but turned back briefly to say, 'Oh, and don't waste bullets, García. One each.'

I nodded at him.

It took all my strength to control my voice as I gave

my men their orders. We had corralled the prisoners at one end of the square and led a line out into the centre. The prisoners had realized what was happening, but seeing our numbers were so great, understood that any attempt to escape would be futile.

I could see how uncomfortable my men were with their task, so I decided that I should fire the first shot. I ordered the most senior Republican out in front of the rest and took my pistol from its holster. My enemy stood tall in front of me. He looked noble in front of his men. I unclipped the safety catch on my gun, noticing how badly my hands shook, and knew that the only way to mask my fear was to act quickly.

Dispelling all thoughts of morals, I lifted my gun to the back of his head and pulled the trigger. The man crumpled at my feet.

'Fire!' I instructed my men.

The shots rang out and the line of men fell. Shouts and screams came from the remaining prisoners as my soldiers dragged the bodies into the corner of the plaza. As they brought out the next line of men, a lone voice could be heard. One man had begun singing the 'Himno de Riego'. His voice trembled, but his fellow men quickly joined in the Republican anthem.

Soon, the force of the other voices gave them strength and they'd sung over the sounds of the gunshots as more of their men had fallen.

'Soldiers, the country calls us to the fight. Let us swear for her to conquer or to die.'

I let them sing. They sang to the very last man. And when the singing of that accursed song had stopped, we piled the final bodies in the corner of the plaza and moved further on into the city. By then, I was a different man.

When we reached the bullring, we discovered killing on a much larger scale. Men and women, soldiers and civilians were mown down in front of my eyes. Not all of them had been killed outright, and the sounds of the dying had turned my stomach.

But I presented myself to the nearest officer and we soon were recruited into the massacre. Since that day, killing has become easier. Now, I have no compunction in bringing death to my enemy. It is my duty: I do it for my country, for Franco and for God.

The gale continues to roar across the dry, barren land and blows grit from the edge of the ditch into my eyes and mouth. Suddenly, I notice the sound has changed. As I close my eyes and listen carefully, I realize it is not the wind making the noise at all.

Opening my eyes, I search the road behind us. And there, behind a whirl of dust, is an enemy armoured car rattling at speed towards us. I shout at my men, who turn and begin firing.

But the machine gun is facing the wrong way. As Luis struggles to move it, I see a man wearing overalls and a beret lean out of the moving vehicle, aim and fire at my gunner. The bullet hits its target, killing Luis instantly, as the two men beside him dive to the bottom of the ditch.

I gasp briefly, but quickly make myself focus on the situation. I shout my orders. Half of the men are to shoot at the truck as it hurtles along the dusty road; the bullets bounce off the armoured car, but my men continue to fire. The others are to get the machine gun cleaned up and ready it to use again. I turn my back to the body slumped in the ditch. I have come to terms with the realities of war, but have no wish to look at Luis's corpse.

We watch as the vehicle drives alongside us on the road, veering off suddenly towards the mound. There it stops, aims its guns towards us and starts firing again. The soldier standing beside me is too slow to duck behind the ditch edge and is hit in the neck. He falls beside me, grasping at his throat as blood bubbles out of the open wound. He turns his head towards me and reaches out to me. For a moment, I want to take his hand, but I stop myself.

I lean instead out of his reach. I glance away to avoid the pitiful look on his face. Thankfully, it is over quickly and his eyes glaze as he drops to the ground.

Through the settling dust, I can see the rescued Republican soldiers running to the rear of the vehicle, where they start to climb in. We carry on shooting, but it's an impossible task, as the truck rains bullets on us.

Then, incredibly, from the dip in the ridge where I am watching, I see one of the fighters run out from beside the truck. I can't believe it — he was safe. What is he doing? His hat is missing and his blond hair is blowing about in the wind. For a moment, it forms a perfect golden halo round his head. He skids to the ground by the edge of the road where one of their men lies. Slinging his gun over his shoulder, he grabs his comrade underneath his arms and starts to drag him towards the truck.

I look along the ditch and see my men are hunched below the ridge, only occasionally firing an aimless shot over their heads. By contrast, the Republicans are now leaning out of their truck firing at us. I watch as the blond soldier reaches the vehicle, and the others grapple the wounded man into it. The blond man then darts out again, weaving across the land back towards the road's edge.

I have had enough. Crouching low, I run along the ditch, instructing my men to cover me. They immediately start firing towards the truck, and I hear the scream of one of the enemy as he is struck. I carry on, scrambling over the body of a soldier I shouted at this morning.

As the ditch becomes more shallow, I sink to my stomach and start crawling. The ditch has curved towards the road, and I am now quite a distance from my men. Peeking above the edge, on my right I can see my men firing at the truck, which is now on my left. The *Rojos* have not seen me, and as I turn towards the road, I see the blond man kneeling by another fallen soldier.

But this time, he is shaking the soldier, shouting at him. It is clear that the man is dead. I lift my pistol. As I watch, the blond repeats the dead man's name: 'Ramón! Ramón!' Distressed, he runs his fingers through his fringe, pulling the hair off his face.

Spotting my moment, I rise to my knees, aim and fire. The bullet hits the blond in the chest and he falls slowly to the road's edge, a surprised look on his face. Diving back behind the ridge, a barrage of bullets hit the ground around me. I crawl as fast as I can back to my men, who have managed to set up the machine gun again and are firing at the vehicle.

As I reach my men, the armoured truck starts up and, with a lurch and a cloud of dust, rattles back to the road and roars away. My men cheer and slap me on the back. I do not approve of this disrespectful behaviour, but they have, in the main, been brave, so I indulge them in their celebration. They know I have made my point about trying to rescue fallen comrades. It may be loyal, it may be seen as courageous, but it is stupid and futile.

The dust of the armoured vehicle can just be seen in the distance as we scout across the land checking bodies. Occasional shots ring out as the wounded are despatched.

I am just walking round the mound the renegades were hiding behind when I see one of our trucks coming towards us, trundling along the road from the town. The lorry slows down as the driver sees me, but I wave him on — we don't need him, and the *Rojos* ahead will be long gone.

As he drives past, I see the boy who struck me at the churchyard sitting in the cab beside the driver. But he does not see me. He is staring, wide-eyed, at the blond fighter lying by the roadside.

The truck rumbles on as I walk over to the fallen soldier. Standing over him, I wonder if he is German or English. His silky hair has fallen back and reveals a young face with freckles scattered over a pointed nose. I look down at his scruffy, mismatched uniform: the half-turned-up shirt collar, missing jacket buttons and torn trousers. Sneering at his lack of pride in his uniform, I lift my pistol, aim at his forehead and fire.

Chapter Five

The train softly jigged the small boy in his seat as he tried to navigate the orange segment into his mouth. He looked up at Alberto watching him and giggled. Alberto smiled back. When Rosa had asked Tino if he'd like to go away with his apu, he'd been thoughtful for a while, then asked if Papá would know he wasn't there. His mother had said when he asked, she'd tell him Tino was on an adventure with Apu. At that, the boy had thought some more, then suddenly seemed to make a decision. Yes, he'd said, he wanted to go.

They'd organized the trip quickly, and although he was clearly a little anxious, Tino had chattered as he helped Alberto pack a lunch to eat on the train. Early the next morning, after an hour's journey by bus, they had left the coast and reached the city. There, they bought tickets at the bustling station and found their train's platform.

Alberto had travelled a few times by rail, but the sleek white train they boarded was like transportation that had been sent from the future. The seats were comfortable, but the window was one large sealed unit that could not be opened. Alberto disliked the air-conditioning and felt ill at ease in the modern bullet shooting through the countryside. But the boy loved it and dashed from one window to the other, pointing out sights to his grandfather. There – a sunflower field. There – a church tower. There – a wind farm.

Alberto looked at the wind farm. Row upon row of tall white wind turbines slowly rotated against the backdrop of a cyan sky. Alberto remembered the old wooden windmill on a farm where he had worked when he was young. For a while, he trawled through his memories trying to locate where the farm had been, but he couldn't remember. He shook his head – if he couldn't remember facts from when he was a young man, how would he remember anything from his childhood?

Some time later, a metallic voice announced a station. Alberto leant over the boy and gently woke him. He had been exhausted by his excitement and had fallen asleep, his head leaning against the large window. Alberto gave him a nod and stood up, swinging his small bag over his shoulder.

As the train silently slowed to a standstill, they waited by the door, which suddenly slid open in front of them. Stepping out into the dry heat, Alberto took a deep breath and looked around. They were in a small town, but judging by the cranes all around, it would quickly become a larger one.

They walked along the platform as the train doors

shut with a quiet clunk and the machine moved off with a hiss. They crossed the modern station of glass and brown brick, out onto the street. It was close to siesta time, so the streets were quiet, the shops pulling down their shutters.

Alberto walked over to a bus stop and squinted at the timetable behind the Perspex. When Tino came over to look, his grandfather showed him where they were going, and together they looked up the time. The bus was not regular, but luckily they only had half an hour to wait. They went back into the station, where a small cafe was open, and Alberto had a coffee, while the boy sucked chocolate milk through a straw. Then the boy took himself to the toilet and Alberto lit a cigarette. Watching Tino ambling back from the bathroom, looking in the counter at the ice creams and humming, the old man knew his decision to get away for a few days had been right.

The bus chugged wearily up the hill. When it reached the top, Alberto and Tino looked over the rolling countryside, covered with bottle-green trees. In front of them, the road snaked through the hills into the distance. As the bus eased downwards, Alberto saw a break in the trees and a large terracotta roof.

A little further on, a wide turn-off appeared on the side of the road and the bus slowed, then stopped. Alberto saw a small wooden sign that read, HACIENDA LOS ZORROS.

'Señor!' called the bus driver to his only passengers. 'Your stop.'

As Alberto stood and ushered the boy in front of him, the driver turned to them and explained, 'Los Zorros is the name of this mountain. There used to be many foxes in these hills. They say it was all you could hear at night – like an orchestra of screams. But in the war . . .' He looked at the child and then up to Alberto. 'Well, in the war, it got too busy round here, so the foxes took their orchestra elsewhere,' he smiled, chuckling.

Tino didn't really understand the joke but smiled at the driver as he climbed off the bus.

'Thank you,' said Alberto to the driver, and they nodded knowingly at each other.

As the bus rattled off, the old man and the boy stood at the end of a long dirt road. It disappeared into the tall trees' dark arches.

'Apu?'

'Yes.'

'Do you remember this?'

'Yes.'

As they walked out of the bright sun and into the mottled light of the pathway, the boy took his grand-father's hand. The old man found the shaded path unnerving – it was as if memories lurked in the shadows. Holding the child's hand reassured them both.

Birds squawked and cawed high above them, and occasionally they heard a small rustle in the bushes nearby. Although Alberto recalled this wood, it was different now. When he was a child, any bird or rabbit was a meal. The hunting had been intense until the woods were eerily silent, bereft of wildlife – even foxes.

The path bent round to the right, and suddenly they came across a large metal gate locked with an enormous padlock. Alberto stopped and looked at the gate, then at the boy.

'I think someone is telling us not to come in,' he said.

Tino scowled. 'We can't give up already, Apu. We've come such a long way.'

Alberto shrugged and was considering climbing over it when the child suddenly slipped past him to the end of the gate, where he slid easily between the metal post and a gorse bush.

'Come on, Apu – it's easy,' Tino said to him from the other side of the gate.

Alberto sighed and eased himself round the edge of the gate, scratching his trousers on the prickly gorse.

On the other side of the gate, they walked further, and the light grew dimmer as the trees overhead became more dense. But after a while, they saw the path open out ahead, bathed in sunlight. As they walked out, they blinked up at the imposing white building in front of them. The high walls reached up to a roof covered in burnt-orange tiles. Bright red geraniums sat on small windowsills, creating splashes of colour against the clean white walls. A solid-oak door sported iron studs, and a black grille lay open against the wall to the left of the door.

They stepped out onto the driveway, which swept in a circle at the front of the house. In the centre, on a carpet of bright green grass, stood an old stone fountain, water trickling lazily from a nymph's mouth.

On the edge of the drive, and on either side of the house, lay carefully manicured gardens featuring red and yellow flowers.

As Alberto looked at the healthy plants with approval, a man carrying a hoe appeared from the side of the house. Looking up with surprise, he crossed the gravel drive towards the old man and small boy.

'Good afternoon, señor,' he said respectfully. 'Can I help you?'

Alberto looked up at the imposing house again, staring for some time.

'Sir?' asked the man.

'I'm sorry,' said Alberto. 'I haven't been here for many years. Can I ask about the owner?'

'Yes, yes. Don García still lives here,' replied the man enthusiastically. 'Of course he is very elderly now, but he has so few visitors, I'm sure he will be delighted to see you both.'

Their footsteps echoed on the terracotta-tiled floor as they followed the housekeeper through the house. The gardener had introduced them to his wife, who looked after the house and the elderly gentleman owner. She did not seem to share her husband's enthusiasm for the don's visitors, but agreed to take them to him.

Her rubber-soled shoes were silent as she led them through high-ceilinged rooms filled with heavy oak furniture and antique rugs.

The señora stopped in front of two large panelled doors and spoke quietly to Alberto. 'Don García does not hear very well these days, so speak loudly and clearly. He is also not comfortable with children, so I'd ask your grandson only to speak when spoken to, which is unlikely. And I suggest you do not detain the señor for too long – for all our sakes.'

Alberto did not understand her last comment, but nodded to the woman, who turned the handle and slowly swung the giant doors open.

The boy grabbed Alberto's hand as they stepped into the dark room. Heavy curtains, which blocked out most of the sunlight, hung partially closed at the long windows. The housekeeper gently pulled the doors shut behind her and they stood still in the musty-smelling room.

Muskets and pistols hung on the walls, and the chimneybreast was decorated with a selection of sabres and swords. On the opposite wall hung an enormous, elaborately framed painting of Christ on the cross, weeping women at his feet, his wounds bleeding profusely and his pain palpable.

Alberto was mesmerized by the painting until he felt a sharp tug at his hand. He glanced down at the boy, who was biting his lip and staring. Alberto followed his gaze. A man so ancient he was barely more than a skeleton sat in a wheelchair in the gloomiest corner of the room. What was left of his white hair was parted sharply, and he had a patchy but precisely trimmed moustache. He was dressed in a dark, tailored suit, too large for his shrunken frame, and his shoes were brightly polished. Medals adorned his jacket, glinting as he reached down and with great effort began to wheel himself towards them.

When he was a few feet from Alberto, he stopped and, breathing deeply, said in a sharp, rasping voice, 'Can I help you?'

'Don García' — Alberto bowed his head slightly — 'my name is Alberto Romero, and this is my grandson.'

The old man nodded graciously at Alberto, ignoring Tino. 'And why are you here?'

'Señor, many years ago, I lived in this house. My grandson and I have come in search of some information about those times.'

'You lived in this house before me?'

'Yes, señor. It was during the time of the war.'

'The war?'

'That's right.'

'Many say that was a bad time for Spain, eh?'

'Yes,' said Alberto.

'And you? What is your opinion of the war?'

Alberto paused for a moment but answered, 'I was just a boy. Those times have passed. I believe it is better to look forward.'

'Hmm. You say you lived here before I moved here?'

'Yes, that's right.'

Don García sucked audibly on his teeth and ran his thumb and forefinger over his moustache before pointing an emaciated finger at Alberto. 'So you were an orphan?'

Alberto nodded slowly.

'A child of *Rojos*, no doubt.'

'I don't know,' said Alberto carefully. 'I don't remember my parents.'

'Mmm,' said the old man, sceptically.

'So, señor, you didn't visit the house during the war years?'

'No. I was too busy ridding the country of red filth,' sneered the man.

Alberto winced.

Pausing for a moment, he persisted, 'Could I ask when you moved here?'

'Franco himself bequeathed me this house. For my services in the war,' said the old man, tapping his medals. 'Those were the days,' he continued. 'The Franco years. Spain was blooming. Since he's been gone, the country has gone to the dogs – don't you agree?'

Alberto stood silent.

'Eh? Don't you agree?'

'I like being able to choose my government,' said Alberto deliberately.

At this, the ancient man started to laugh a wheezing laugh, but quickly began to gasp for breath. His wheezing soon turned to coughing that shook his entire bony body.

Alberto took a step towards him, but the old man lifted his papery face and scorned, 'Socialist rubbish!'

Alberto heard the boy gasp quietly, and squeezed his hand reassuringly.

'The country's run by snivelling, weak populists. And do you know who is to blame for this country's fall? Do you know who is the traitor?' He paused to take a breath, his watery eyes on Alberto. 'The king!'

With this, Don García began to cough again. He pulled a clean white handkerchief from his top pocket and coughed violently into it, crumpling in his chair.

Alberto began walking towards the door, pulling the riveted child with him.

'I think we will leave you now, señor,' he said firmly.

But as he reached for the door handle, the venomous voice rasped, 'He betrayed Franco – the hero who saved this country from godlessness. He prepared the king to take the reins. And how was he repaid? With treachery. The king turned his back on Franco and all that he stood for.'

Alberto turned to look at the ancient man.

'If the king were to walk into this house right now, do you know what I would do?' García paused, gulping small mouthfuls of air. 'I would spit in his face,' he hissed.

Alberto blinked at the wheezing body in the wheelchair, a wisp of a memory flickering in front of him, gone before he could grasp it. Then, turning quickly, he yanked the door open, grabbed Tino's arm and steered him out of the room. Without speaking, he marched through the house, the boy scampering to keep up.

When they reached the main door, Alberto stepped out into the sunshine and took a deep breath. He turned his face up to the sun and, still breathing deeply, rubbed his chest.

Suddenly, he folded over with a soft groan.

'Apu!' cried Tino, grabbing hold of his leg.

'Señor,' shouted the gardener. He dropped his hoe and dashed towards him.

Alberto lifted his hand to calm him and slowly stood up straight. His face was ashen and he let the gardener take his arm and lead him to a garden bench, where he sat down heavily.

The gardener called into an open window. When his wife's face appeared, he asked her to bring some water.

'Thank you,' said Alberto when he had his breath back. Looking into the gardener's worried face, he smiled and said, 'I'm fine. I just had a shock.'

He turned to the boy, who was on the verge of tears. Alberto reached out and touched his cheek. 'Don't worry, Tino. It will take more than a wicked old man to finish me off.'

Not for the first time, Alberto wondered if he'd done the right thing bringing the boy on this journey.

'Ah. Don García is on ferocious form today, is he?' asked the gardener. 'I'm sorry. I should have warned you. My wife calls me a fool, but it is in my blood to respect my elders, no matter how terrible they are.'

'He *is* a fool,' huffed the housekeeper as she approached with a large glass of water. 'He can't see that the old man is a snake, through and through. It's no wonder he's on his own — and has been all these years.'

Alberto thanked her for the water and gulped it down.

'My husband is only grateful to him,' continued the housekeeper, 'because he kept his father in employment after the war. His father was a cripple and Don García was cruel to him all his life. But in a time when work was scarce, it was a job, and Papá Jorge could feed his children.'

'My father used to bring me here to help him when his walking became very bad,' continued the gardener. 'And when my father passed away, Don García let me carry on his work. I've worked here all my life. The old man is very particular about the garden, but I think his attention to detail shows.'

Alberto nodded. 'I admired your work when we arrived. The flowers are beautiful.'

'This was all vegetable gardens when my father was here. He had to feed over a hundred orphans during the war. He worked very hard in those years.'

'Yes, I remember,' said Alberto quietly.

'Oh!' cried the gardener. 'You were an orphan here?'

Alberto nodded.

'Do you remember my father?'

'A little,' replied Alberto, squinting. 'We weren't allowed to spend time with anyone like that, but I remember a man with a limp working outside. And a kind woman who prepared our meals – I can't recall her name.'

'Isabel!' stated the gardener proudly.

'Yes,' said Alberto, pleased. 'Señorita Isabel.'

'She left here at the end of the war. She married and went to live in her husband's town. I believe she still runs the restaurant there.'

'Oh,' gasped the boy. 'Apu, maybe Señora Isabel will remember you.'

Alberto looked at Tino, then back to the gardener. 'Is it far from here?'

'It's a few hours' drive. It used to take most of a day to get there, but the new *autopista* makes it a much faster journey. There's a bus that leaves in the morning.'

'In the morning?' repeated Alberto.

'Yes. And if you have nowhere to stay tonight, we would be honoured if you would stay with us.'

'Oh no,' said Alberto quickly, 'we could not impose. If you could direct us to a *hostería*—'

'Nonsense,' replied the gardener's wife sternly. 'You have both had a shock, thanks to that nasty old man. This boy looks quite exhausted. My husband will take

67

you home with him now, while I see to Don García. He has a nurse here during the night, but I'll give him something to make him sleep before I go. He's upset enough people today.'

Taking the glass from Alberto, she patted the boy's head before returning into the house.

'Right,' said the gardener, 'I'll just tidy up my tools.'

As the gardener walked away, Tino turned to his grandfather.

Alberto smiled at him. 'Perhaps Isabel will know something, eh?'

His grandson grinned as he threw his arms around his apu and hugged him tightly.

Chapter Six

MICHAEL
6 March 1937

I carefully fold the thin pages and slide them into the envelope. Sniffing the envelope, I remember how it smelt of June's perfume when it first arrived. Now, it smells of dirt. I tuck it into my top pocket and lean back against the ditch, looking up at the inky twilight sky. A short distance away, some of the men are singing softly.

What will she be doing now? Helping her mum wash up after tea, perhaps. Listening to the wireless with her brother. Maybe she's sitting at her father's desk, pushing that glorious auburn hair off her face as she writes me another letter.

I have no idea how many letters have gone astray, but each one that makes it to me is precious. I've read all of them so many times I know every word, every scratch of her pen, every smile or tear that accompanies the words. Half of the Spaniards I'm fighting with are illiterate, but they understand love, and they wink at me when they see me with June's letters.

'*And I say thank you to the Señor for the women. Yes, the women and the wine . . .*' sings a smooth, heavily accented Spanish voice, and I see Ramón stroll towards me in the gloom.

'*Amigo,*' I say, 'what's happening?'

'Nothing yet,' replies Ramón as he eases himself down beside me. 'We'll leave once it's dark.'

'Righto,' I say in English.

'Rrrighto,' mimics Ramón with his rolling tongue.

'Shut up,' I tell him in Spanish as he chuckles deeply.

'Rubio,' says Ramón, 'life does not always need to be so serious.'

'Ramón,' I reply sternly, 'there are many serious issues I am concerned about.'

At this, Ramón sighs deeply, waiting for me to begin one of our long political and ideological discussions.

'Serious issues,' I continue, 'such as how much you need a bath.'

'Ha!' roars Ramón, throwing an arm around me. 'This is the serious issue: where will I find the next bottle of wine and beautiful pair of eyes?'

Laughing, we both look up and observe the blanket of stars that has appeared above us. I imagine that Ramón is thinking of the dark-haired señoritas he will woo with tales of fighting the Fascists and life on the road.

Not for the first time, I am struck by how different we are and how even so we are such good friends. Ramón is from the Basque Country. His family have been farmers there for as long as anyone can remember.

Ramón has a wife, four children and a farm full of pigs, which I truly believe he adores more than the children. He is a devout, if selective, Catholic. A naturally happy man, he finds the good in every situation.

When the Fascists launched their revolt across Spain last summer, Ramón joined a peasants' militia to defend the government. He tells me the fighting had been hard around his homeland for many months, but the Republicans had held the enemy at bay. Word of his courage and inspirational leadership had quickly spread, and he had been called to Madrid by central command. At first, he refused, stating that he fought for the autonomous Basque government. But when Franco proclaimed himself *generalísimo* at the end of September, Ramón had realized he was fighting for freedom from fascism. We met in Madrid last November, when I'd first arrived.

'Miguel,' says Ramón softly. I turn to look at him. He rarely calls me by my name. Instead, he and the men call me 'El Rubio', the Blond, because they're not used to seeing such fair colouring.

Still watching the darkening sky, he continues, 'Miguel, I have a bad feeling. Deep in my stomach. I have a very bad feeling.'

I study his face.

His beret pulls back his black hair, exposing strong, rounded features despite a scruffy beard. His mouth, always so quick to smile and laugh, is set in a serious line. I've never heard him speak like this.

I mull over his comment. Ramón is deeply superstitious, and I know there is little I can do to persuade him his feeling is most likely a simple psychological reaction to our situation.

Eventually, I reply, 'It's probably José's cooking.'

Ramón snorts with laughter and turns to me. He knows we can't let his feeling affect us or infect the other men. He reaches into his pocket and pulls out a pack of cigarettes. When he offers, I take one – I'm getting used to the coarse flavour. We smoke in silence as the light fades and the singing becomes quieter.

Stubbing out the cigarette, Ramón puffs one last cloud of smoke. Rising to his feet, he looks over to the men, who are starting to gather their packs.

'It's time,' he says, and reaching a hand down to me, he smiles, '*Vamanos, muchacho*.'

Smiling, I let him pull me up.

The quiet tramping of boots on the dusty road is suddenly interrupted by an almighty fart.

As we all groan, Felipe whispers loudly, 'Hellfire, José! It is not the Nationalists that will be the end of me – it is your beans, goddamit!'

'The noise alone will lead them to us,' comes Ramón's voice from the dark. The moon is slim tonight and there's little light on the road.

'*Hombres*,' replies José, 'you're missing the point. I have given you a secret weapon. With just one bowl of my beans, you could blow up an enemy truck.'

As we snigger, Martín sighs. 'Oh, what I would give for a plate of lamb chops and a cup of cider.'

'Beef stew for me,' says Víctor. 'With my Patricia's bread to mop up the sauce.'

'Men, men,' states Ramón, 'you have not eaten great food until you have tasted my sausages. I know about pigs and I can tell you that a happy pig makes a tasty sausage—'

'Fish and chips,' I interrupt, before Ramón gets carried away talking about his pigs.

'Ha,' scoffs Martín, 'the English are not famous for their food.'

'Ah, Martín, you would love it. Imagine the very best calamari batter — thick and crunchy. Bite through that and inside is soft, steaming fish. And served with it, deep-fried potatoes, with vinegar splashed over them.'

'Vinegar?' I hear Ramón sneer.

'One day, Ramón, I'll take you to the finest fish and chip shop in Liverpool. Then you'll see,' I reply, smiling to myself. For a moment, I can smell the vinegar and hear the bubbling of the fat, and it makes me think of time spent with June.

I first met her when she came into the bookshop, looking for Orwell's *Burmese Days*. As I searched for it, I'd made a comment about British imperialism. In a flash, she had disputed my opinion and accused me of utopianism. Before I knew it, we'd been talking politics for half an hour and she'd had to dash back to the solicitor's office where she worked.

She had left so quickly she had forgotten to take the book. So when she came back the next day, I'd wrapped her book in brown paper and mentally prepared a speech to ask her out. She'd smiled a slightly crooked smile that I had already come to adore and agreed. That Saturday, we went for a long walk in the damp cold and ended up at the steamy fish and chip shop, where we drank endless cups of tea and talked. As I watched her blow on her vinegar-drenched chips, I knew I had fallen for her.

'I think it sounds delicious,' says a young voice.

'Emilio, is that you?' I gasp. I turn to the indistinguishable figure that spoke.

'Yes, it's me,' replies the youngster.

'Emilio, you're supposed to be securing the flanks.'

'Pah!' he retorts. 'There's no one else on this road — we'd all see a vehicle approaching. All I'm doing is walking into farts.'

Sighing, I reach for Emilio's shadowy arm and pull him to one side.

'Ramón,' I say quietly, 'we'll see you at the next break.'

'Rrrighto, Rubio,' comes the reply.

I know that Emilio is young: he claims to be eighteen, although I think he's closer to sixteen. But the teaching of modern warfare skills is one of the reasons I'm with this group. However, it seems no matter how I try to instil a sense of professionalism in them, the Spanish sense of relaxed optimism always triumphs.

As we fall back from the rest of the group, I gently explain again how important it is to protect the rear. I remind him to use all of his senses, and how to hold his gun ready. I can sense Emilio's sulkiness as I also instruct him not to smoke when he's marking the rear. He sucks on his cigarette and the glowing end casts an orange glimmer across his sullen face.

Walking quietly, I listen to the cicadas, and in the far distance, a dog barks. The air smells faintly of mimosa. The night has a chill to it and I pull up my collar. Emilio finishes his cigarette and I hear him flick the butt towards the bushes on the roadside.

Suddenly, I hear a rustle. Emilio hears it too and we both stop, holding our breath and looking into the darkness. The noise came from where Emilio's cigarette must have landed. It's probably just an animal, but I lift my gun.

When no further noise comes, we edge slowly towards the bushes. Although I can see nothing, I can sense something. An animal would have scampered off as soon as it heard anything large approach. Gently pushing Emilio to the left, I step towards the right of the bushes.

'Show yourself,' I state loudly.

We stand, waiting and alert, but nothing happens.

I'm just about to repeat myself when leaves suddenly rustle and twigs crack. I can just make out the small figure that emerges from behind the outline of the bush.

'Come here!' I say forcefully, trying to hide my confusion.

I hear Emilio shift his gun as the figure wrestles its way out of the bushes. As the black shape makes its way towards me, I reach into my pocket and pull out my lighter.

'Stop there!' I snap when the figure is a few feet from me.

I flick the flint and a fat flame bursts from the lighter. I lower it towards the shadowy form and Emilio and I find ourselves staring at a small boy. He is filthy and dishevelled, with bits of twig and leaves sticking out of his hair.

I drop to my haunches.

'Be careful — it may be some kind of decoy,' whispers Emilio earnestly.

'What's your name?' I ask the child, ignoring Emilio.

'Alberto,' comes the whispered reply.

'How did you get here?'

'I walked.'

'Where from?'

At this, I see the child's chin tremble; then his face crumples and tears start to roll down his cheeks. I drop my gun, pull the boy into my body and hug him hard. Feeling the child sob into my chest, I try to decide the best course of action.

By the time the crying has subsided to muffled snuffling, I've made up my mind.

'Emilio, take the boy ahead to the unit. Tell them to break early. We'll get the boy a cup of tea and look at the map — let's see if we can drop him off somewhere safe.'

'Yes, sir,' says Emilio. At last, he is responding to an order. I hope it's not too dark for the child to see me smile at him. Then I stand and let Emilio take Alberto's hand to lead him off.

By the time I reach the unit, they have built a small fire and are heating some water. Ramón is doing piglet impressions for the child, who giggles at the silliness. The other men look on, smiling.

For an instant, it strikes me that it is this compassion that we are fighting for. The Fascists have no time for kindness, only power and discipline. We believe in supporting the poorest and a fairer life for all. And yet, it is this compassion that could be our downfall.

Dispelling such an unsettling thought, I sit on a rock by the fire. Ramón sees me and, placing his beret on the boy's head, passes him to Emilio.

'So, Rubio,' he says, crossing to me, 'I see you are still recruiting fighters. Don't you think this one is a little young?'

I smile and accept a cup of weak tea from José.

'Did you find out where he came from?' I ask.

'Emilio asked. He can't remember anything. He doesn't know the name of his village or what family he has. The only thing he remembers is his name — Alberto Romero. And a car. He says he remembers a car. He says he's been walking and walking but has no idea for how long.'

'Poor kid. Any idea what we can do with him?'

Felipe hands Ramón the map and he points a dirty finger to a small town.

'This is the nearest place that we know has plenty of Republican support. There are no reports of Nationalists there yet. The best thing to do is take him to the Church – they will look after him.'

I give Ramón a steady stare.

'The Church?' I ask, incredulous.

'Rubio,' replies Ramón curtly, 'this is not the time to have a discussion about religion. No matter what the Church is doing politically, when it comes to situations like this, they will show mercy to a lost child.'

'Suffer the little children, Ramón?' I spit. 'If we leave him in a *Rojo* village, they will assume he is a *Rojo* child. I know you don't want to believe the Church could hurt a child, but there is no guarantee he will be safe. I think we should try to get him to the Red Cross. They may even evacuate him. At least there won't be any fat, barbaric bishops on a religious crusade against—'

'Enough!' hollers Ramón, raising his hand. 'He will be safe with the Church.' Then he drops his hand and speaks softly. 'Do not forget our mission. We have a long way to travel and we cannot make a detour to find the Red Cross. At least if he is taken into an organization like the Church, they may be able to find his family.'

I know Ramón struggles with an inner conflict – his

genuine faith versus a greedy, self-serving Church — and perhaps I am pushing him too far. I take a moment; then, reluctantly, I nod. 'You're right.'

I know he will not be swayed in this matter, and despite our friendship, he is the leader of this unit and I must respect his orders.

We return to the map and plan what to do. It is agreed I will take the boy to the village. It's still early, so I should be able to leave him at the church and then get back to the unit before daybreak.

As I gulp down the last of my tea, I turn to José. 'Is there any food for the boy? He needs something to eat. Anything but your beans.'

'Alberto, are you sure you can't remember anything about your home?' I press as we walk along the edge of a field. We split from the other men an hour ago, and they followed the road, while the boy and I cut across the fields to get to the town.

'No, nothing,' says the boy.

'Not even your mamá?'

'No,' says Alberto a little hesitantly.

'What?' I urge gently. 'Is there something you remember? Anything at all?'

'Yes, but it's not Mamá,' he replies thoughtfully. 'It's Mimi.'

'Well, that's a start. Maybe she's an aunt or a friend. What do you think?'

Alberto is quiet as we step through the grass.

'I don't know. I just remembered the name,' he eventually admits.

'Never mind,' I say encouragingly. 'I'm sure it will come back soon, and then someone will be able to take you home.'

We walk in silence for a while, before Alberto starts hesitantly, 'Why—' then stops.

'Why what?' I say. 'Come on.'

'Why do they call you "El Rubio"?' he asks shyly.

'Aha!' I say cheerfully. 'Look at this!' At that, I whip off my black hat and my fair hair flops out. The night's clouds have cleared and I know in the moonlight the blond can be seen – like a golden halo, Ramón often remarks sarcastically. If I'd been at home, June would have trimmed it for me, but I haven't given haircuts much thought lately.

The boy gasps.

'Have you ever seen hair this yellow before?' I ask.

'No, never.'

'Where I live, it's not unusual. In fact, it's really very ordinary.'

'Don't you live in Spain?' asks the boy.

'Well, I do now, but only because of the war. I'm from another country, called England. Have you heard of it?' I put my hat back on, tucking in as much hair as I can.

'Yes, I think so.'

'Well, maybe you learnt about it at school,' I suggest. I hope it will jog a memory.

'I don't know,' says the boy quietly. 'Is that why you talk funny?'

I laugh. 'Yes. It's because usually I talk English. I'm from a city called Liverpool. It's near the ocean and is a famous port. My uncle was a sailor. He married a Spanish lady and brought her back home with him. My aunt María taught me Spanish, and whenever I was at her house, playing with my cousins, we would speak Spanish. And now I speak it every day, but I'll always sound a bit different because it's not my native language.'

'Are you a sailor too?'

'No!' I laugh at the thought. And yet, here I am, a soldier. 'My father has a bookshop. I worked there before I came to Spain. I used to live above the shop with my parents.'

For a moment, I wonder how the bookshop is doing. While I was working with my father, I persuaded him to build up a section of political books. I had been keen because I was so interested in current affairs and politics myself. I had also known it would bring in the union and party leaders, and the sales would be good for business. Dad had been reluctant at first, but soon we had stocked everything from Marx and Lenin to Mussolini's autobiography, and had become well known for our range.

One of the regulars at the bookshop was John, a unionist down at the docks. He had invited me to meetings, where we had listened to speakers talk of the rise of

the Fascists and the danger it posed to the Labour movement. It was with John that I had gone to London and
volunteered last year.

'Why did you come to my country?' asks Alberto.

'Well, it's complicated,' I say cautiously. Perhaps the
boy's family are Nationalists. It's not my place to con-
fuse the child. How do I explain my reasons for coming
to fight?

I hear my father's words ringing in my ears. 'Don't
go,' he'd said. 'It's not your fight.' But I'd always known
I'd fight fascism, ever since I had sat in the cinema and
watched the newsreel showing them burning books in
Germany, works of literature, philosophy and science
all going up in flames. It had sent chills down my spine.
I had known that at some point I would have to stand up
to the indoctrination, the persecution, the ignorance.

'Alberto,' I begin tentatively, 'there are times when
you see someone doing something bad and it makes
you so angry that you have to do something about it. I
think that the Nationalists are doing something terribly
wrong. And even though this is not my country, or my
people, I want to try and make things better, fairer.
I've come to help the Spanish people fight against what
I consider to be unjust and immoral.'

The boy is silent.

'Does that make any sense?' I ask doubtfully, but
looking down, I see that the dark shadow of the child is
not by my side. Glancing back, I see he is standing still
a few feet behind.

'Alberto?'

'I just had a memory,' says the boy softly.

'What was it?'

'I hit another boy.'

'Why?'

'I don't know.'

'Well, that's great! Not great that you're hitting other children, but great that you remember something. Perhaps that's the beginning of your memory coming back.'

The boy is quiet; he seems to be lost in thought.

'Maybe Ramón was right, Alberto,' I say, trying to lift the mood a little. 'Maybe we should take you with us to fight. I bet you've got quite a punch, eh?' I give his shoulder a light tap.

After a pause, he throws a semi-serious punch at my leg.

'Hmm – your technique needs a little work. Look, if you hold your hand like this, you won't hurt your thumb.' I lean down and carefully fold his little hand into a fist. 'And if you're going to hit someone, bring your arm up like this – in a jab. See?'

Alberto jabs his arm quickly and lands a punch on the side of my head. Losing my balance, I fall to the ground heavily.

'Hey,' I say, 'watch what you're doing!' With that, I pull him down and pummel him. He rolls on the ground laughing.

'Who's the champion now, eh?' I ask, tickling the squirming boy. When he's giggling so much he can barely breathe, I stop, worried I might make him sick. As we lie on the grass panting, he rolls towards me and embraces me. I give him a bear hug.

I squeeze Alberto's hand and he turns his face up to me. I lift my finger to my lips and he nods seriously. Although we believe the village to be on the Republican side, our information is often unreliable. And when there's support for both sides, as there is in this region, we cannot rely on anyone for our security.

I bend down so that the boy and I are on the same level; then, as quietly as we can, we start to run. We pass shops and houses, dark and shut up for the night.

A short distance from the main square, I steer Alberto into a doorway, and we stop to catch our breath.

Suddenly, a dog starts barking ferociously on the other side of the door. Instinctively, I put my hand over Alberto's open mouth, but he stops himself from crying out in fear. I drop again and we make a dash to the shadows in the square.

When we reach the outer walls of the church, we edge around it, making our way down a walkway until we come across a gate. In the dim light, I can see a small graveyard inside. Very slowly I turn the handle, and with a small squeak it opens. I usher Alberto in and he stands against the wall, while I quietly shut the gate behind us.

Across the dusty courtyard is a side door into the church itself, with a small bench beside it. We walk across to the bench and I indicate Alberto should sit down. My plan is to leave the child there for the remaining hours of night. The church will open early and they'll discover him. With the Church supporting the Fascists, I can't risk being found by a priest.

Kneeling beside him, I take out one of June's letters. Carefully, I rip the triangle off the back of the envelope. Tucking the envelope back in my pocket, I fish out a pencil and, leaning on my knee, carefully write ALBERTO ROMERO on the white paper.

I tuck the paper into Alberto's jacket pocket and stand up. I've been dreading this moment, and as the small boy looks up at me with his large, round eyes, I have no idea what to say. After a moment, I punch him softly on the shoulder.

'Good luck, mate,' I whisper in English.

Then, with a crack of metal against wood, the door beside us opens, causing light to flood out of the church. Like startled rabbits, Alberto and I stare at a priest in long black robes, framed by the open door. He is tall and spectacled, and looks me straight in the eye. After what seems an age, he turns to Alberto, then back to me.

It seems as if he understands what is happening. He steps out of the church towards Alberto and places a protective hand on his head, then nods firmly at me. This priest is not what I was expecting – I sense he is a man of integrity.

Alberto is watching me nervously. I flash him a wink. He gives me a tiny smile in return. By the time I pull the gate to behind me, the wooden door is shut, with the priest and Alberto inside. The romantic in me notices a small star directly above the church glow a little more brightly.

The pragmatist in me hopes my instincts are right about the priest.

Chapter Seven

'Papá? Is that you?' Alberto's daughter's voice crackled at him down the phone line.

'Yes, it's me. I didn't know if you'd be at the hospital.'

'No, they sent me home. I'm here and Cristina is too. She arrived this morning. Her mother-in-law is looking after her husband and the children.'

'Good. I'm glad your sister is with you. How is Juan Carlos?'

'He's doing much better. In fact, he was speaking a little today. The doctors are very pleased with his progress.'

'That's good news, Rosa,' the old man sighed, relieved. He nodded at the boy, who was looking up expectantly.

'Papá?'

'He's here,' he said, passing the phone to his grandson.

'Mamá?'

As Alberto walked away, he heard the child chattering excitedly to his mother about where they'd been and who they'd met.

He knew how much the boy's mother would be missing her cherished child. Rosa and Juan Carlos had been through many years of heartbreak trying to have a baby. When first her older sister and then her brother's wife had delivered one baby after another, Rosa had been delighted for them. But María Luisa would tell Alberto of the pain their daughter had silently suffered.

Alberto knew María Luisa blamed herself. She had suffered numerous miscarriages, both before the birth of their first child and in between the others. Rosa herself had been born almost eight years after her elder sister. Superstitious, María Luisa thought she had passed this terrible affliction on to her youngest daughter.

Then, when it seemed Rosa and Juan Carlos had given up, Rosa had fallen pregnant. As she blossomed and grew, she remained cautious, reluctant to express her joy. At the birth, there were complications, and María Luisa told Alberto afterwards that for a short time both Rosa and the baby had been in danger. The child was immediately whisked away for special care.

A few days later, Alberto had gone to visit at the hospital. He watched his pale, exhausted daughter sleeping, and then he and his wife went to see the baby. They joined a worried Juan Carlos peering into an incubator.

As Alberto had looked at the pink, wrinkled baby, it squirmed and raised a tiny clenched fist into the air.

'Look at that,' he said to Juan Carlos. 'You have a little fighter there.'

Juan Carlos turned to Alberto and gave him a weary smile.

'He must take after his grandfather,' he replied.

Alberto walked into the kitchen, where the gardener and his wife were sitting drinking coffee and chatting comfortably.

'Thank you for the use of your phone,' said Alberto. 'You must let me give you some money towards the bill.'

'Nonsense,' they said in unison.

'How is your son-in-law?' asked the gardener.

'My daughter says he's doing much better.'

'Oh good,' said the gardener's wife. She poured Alberto a cup of coffee.

Nodding his thanks, Alberto said, 'So, Isabel is running a restaurant now? I'm not surprised. She always fed us as well as she could at the orphanage. I know there was little food in those days.'

'Yes,' replied the gardener. 'My father used to say she could turn an old onion and a bit of sawdust into a hearty meal! That's quite a skill, eh?'

'Yes,' nodded Alberto, smiling.

'We went to visit her when I was very young. As I remember, she married after the war. She went to live in her husband's family's town, and he set up a restaurant in the square. I was little, but I remember her.

'My sister was travelling that way last year and went to see if the restaurant was still there. She said that although her husband had died some years ago, Isabel was healthy and well, and the restaurant was doing better than ever.'

'I'm looking forward to seeing her,' said Alberto. 'I doubt she'll remember me — there were so many of us.'

'It's surprising what people remember,' said the gardener's wife.

Just then the boy walked into the kitchen, beaming.

'I told Mamá we were going to find Apu's birthday tomorrow and she said Papá was getting better.'

Alberto got the feeling there was something Tino hadn't mentioned, but the boy seemed happy.

'Excellent,' said the gardener's wife. 'Now, sit down while I make you some warm milk. Then off to bed — it's late, and tomorrow is another adventure.'

Fields of sunflowers lay like yellow eiderdowns as far as Alberto could see. They had left the pine-tree hills some time ago, and now the bus was travelling down a long, straight, empty road.

Tino was chattering as usual, and Alberto was only half listening, nodding occasionally. He felt an uneasy mixture of feelings. There was the anticipation that Isabel would be able to tell him something of his past. But he also knew it was probable she wouldn't remember him, and this would be the end of the journey. The thought of it being over made him sad.

Nevertheless, it was good to see the countryside again. After the dry coast, filled with foreigners and tall

buildings, it was pleasing to see how familiar the land-
scape was inland. The crops had changed over the
years, and solar panels and wind farms were peppered
across the horizon, but this was the Spain he remembered from his youth. Still and unhurried, colourful
and fertile. He hoped his grandson would remember
this trip when he was older.

An hour later, the bus pulled into a bus stop on the
outer road of a small town. Alberto helped the boy off
the bus and they strolled through the streets. A tiny
supermarket bustled with women. Old men sat outside
a coffee shop smoking, chatting and enjoying the sun.
A lone dog trotted down the pavement, confident in his
destination.

At the end of the road, they found themselves in a
small square framed by a scattering of shops.

'Apu, look,' said the boy, pointing across the square.

Alberto looked and saw an unfussy restaurant with
white walls and a few metal chairs on the pavement
outside. Above the open door, a sign read RESTAURANTE
LOS NIÑOS.

'That must be it,' said Alberto. He took the boy's
hand.

As they walked across the road towards the restaurant, Alberto glanced at the far end of the square. There
stood an old stone church. Its large wooden doors were
open, and in the tower above hung a bell.

A car tooted, breaking Alberto's reverie, and he
realized he was standing in the middle of the road. He

hurried Tino across to the other side, but when they reached the pavement outside the restaurant, he turned once again to look at the church.

'Apu? What is it?'

'Nothing,' said Alberto distractedly. 'It's just . . . that church seems familiar. I don't know this town, but I feel I've seen that church before.'

'Maybe Señora Isabel brought you here,' suggested the boy.

Alberto shook his head, confused. 'I don't think so.'

At length he broke his gaze from the church, shrugged and smiled at the boy. Together, they walked into the restaurant.

A long bar stretched the length of the room, with three large barrels sitting on one end. Smoked ham and bunches of garlic hung from the ceiling, and the walls were covered with paintings of food.

With it being so early, the restaurant was empty. Behind the bar was an open door covered by a beaded curtain. Alberto called a hello towards it.

A tall, greying man stepped through the door, the beads creating the sound of running water as he did so.

'Yes?'

'Excuse me,' said Alberto politely, 'I am looking for Doña Isabel.'

The man looked at them with dark eyes that twinkled as a smile broke over his face.

'Mamá! You have a suitor!' he called over his shoulder.

Tino giggled behind his hand.

'What?' came a shout through the beaded curtain as they heard footsteps on the tiled floor. 'Andrés, what is your silliness this time?' The bead curtain separated and a small, wiry woman with short silver hair stepped out. She used a stick to walk, leaning on it with her right hand.

'Mamá, you have a visitor,' explained Andrés.

Isabel looked at Alberto, her pale eyes almost obscured by large glasses.

'Can I help you?' she asked curiously.

Alberto cleared his throat. He had been planning what he would say on the journey to the town, but now his mouth was dry and his mind a blank.

'Doña Isabel, we have met before. That is to say, a long time ago,' Alberto stammered.

Isabel looked at Alberto patiently. Then she looked at the boy. 'Señor, please sit down. Andrés, bring us some sherry. And something for our young friend here.'

Isabel pointed to a table and the boy dutifully climbed onto a seat. Alberto held a chair out as the elderly woman walked slowly to the table. As she sat down, she sighed, 'I am not as quick as I once was. Old age is a terrible thing.'

As Alberto sat, Isabel turned to the boy and, smiling warmly at him, said, 'Welcome to Los Niños, child. A very long time ago, it was my job to feed lots of children. So when my husband took over this restaurant, he named it Los Niños because he said anyone who walked

93

through the door would be fed as well as possible. Just like the children.'

'My grandpapá was one of the children,' said Tino excitedly.

'What?' Isabel turned from the boy and looked into Alberto's face.

He nodded simply.

At that moment, Andrés arrived at the table carrying a tray. He placed a small glass of chilled sherry in front of his mother, then another in front of Alberto. For the boy, he opened a bottle of lemonade and poured it into a glass. Then he placed a basket of bread and a plate of thinly sliced ham in the middle of the table.

'Is there anything else, Mamá?' he asked kindly.

His mother shook her head.

'I'll take care of the kitchen. Let me know if you need me,' said Andrés. He put a hand softly on his mother's shoulder.

Isabel placed her hand over his, smiling warmly up at him. Alberto noticed some of her fingers were gnarled. While she was probably at least ten years older than him, he had seen his own knuckles and joints swell and knew the ache of arthritis.

As Andrés strolled to the bead curtain, Isabel turned to Alberto.

'Were you at the orphanage?' she asked quietly.

'Yes.'

Slowly, a smile spread across her lips, and behind the glasses, her eyes seemed to flicker with light.

'I always wondered if I would see any of you again.'

'My grandson suggested I make this journey.' Alberto looked at the boy, who grinned widely.

'Eat, child,' said Isabel. She pushed the plate of ham towards him. Still grinning, Tino picked up a sliver of ham and started to gnaw at it as he reached across for a piece of bread.

Isabel turned back to Alberto.

'I apologize for arriving unannounced,' he said. 'This trip was unplanned, and I only heard that you were here yesterday.'

'I am delighted you have come.'

'So am I. Forgive me, but it has been many years and I was unsure if I would recognize you. Now I see you, I know without a doubt it is you.'

'Well, you are at the advantage, señor. I'm afraid I don't remember you.'

Alberto chuckled loudly. 'Of course you don't remember me. I've lost a little hair since the last time you saw me,' he said. He ran a hand over his balding head.

Isabel smiled back at him. 'Perhaps I will remember your name.'

'Alberto. Alberto Romero.'

Isabel gave a small gasp and lifted her hand to her mouth. 'Alberto?'

'Yes. You remember me?'

Isabel took a moment. She carefully smoothed her apron over her black skirt. With a hand that shook

95

slightly, she removed her glasses and laid them in her lap. Alberto could see her eyes were watery.

'I hope I haven't upset you,' he said uncomfortably.

Isabel reached out and patted his hand. 'Alberto,' she answered quietly. 'If it had not been for you, I would not have met my husband.'

Confused, Alberto looked at Isabel, unsure what to say. The boy, sitting on the edge of his seat and watching them intently, sipped his drink and reached for another piece of bread.

'How . . . ?' started Alberto.

'My husband was in the army. For most of the war, he drove lorries, moving supplies. One day, he and his lorry brought you to the orphanage. That was the first time we met. After that, he found ways to visit whenever he could. Sometimes he brought extra supplies to help me feed you all. Sometimes he only brought his smiling eyes. But that was enough.

'He wanted to marry me long before the end of the war, but I didn't want to leave the children. By the time the war finished, there were so many orphans that the Church arranged for the orphanage to be closed, and the children to be moved to an institution in the city.'

Alberto nodded.

'I stayed to help clean the house for the next owner; then my husband and I married and moved here. He left the army and we took over the restaurant. I did all the cooking, and my husband looked after the customers. It was difficult — there was so little food, and soon I had Andrés – but we managed. And every year on our anniversary, my husband and I would raise a glass in thanks to the small boy who rarely spoke, but who brought us together.'

Isabel smiled, and patted Alberto's hand again.

'I'm pleased to have been of service,' Alberto said, a little embarrassed. 'And I'm sorry your husband is not here. I would have liked to have met him – again.'

'And he would have been pleased to meet you too. How did you find me?'

'We went to the old orphanage. The gardener there is the son of the gardener during the war.'

'Of course, Jorge's family. Are they well?'

'Very well. And now my grandson and I are hoping to continue on to discover more of my childhood. I'm afraid I have no memories of the time before my arrival at the orphanage. Did your husband ever tell you where he brought me from?'

'Here!' said Isabel, tapping the table. 'This village.'

'Apu, that's why you remember the church,' interrupted Tino excitedly.

'Yes,' agreed Isabel. 'You were at the church. My husband came to visit his family, and when the priest saw his lorry, he asked him to take you somewhere safe. The fighting was getting closer and the priest was worried that the church would be in danger.'

'I remember,' said Alberto quietly. He looked into the distance. 'Yes, I remember a priest.'

'By the time I came to live in the town, he was gone.

Some said he was taken away by soldiers, but there were many rumours and recriminations at that time. I would have liked to have thanked him.'

Alberto nodded thoughtfully.

'I'm afraid I don't know any more,' said Isabel apologetically.

'No, you have been very helpful. You see, I have only tiny flashes of memory — like the church and the priest — but nothing of my family.'

Isabel shook her head sadly. 'You barely spoke when you arrived. So many children had seen such terrible things — it's hardly surprising they didn't want to talk about it.'

Alberto sipped his sherry thoughtfully.

'Why don't you visit the church?' suggested Isabel. 'They may have records of your arrival. And maybe they know what happened to the priest. I'm afraid I can't remember his name.'

'Yes, Apu — let's go and visit the church,' the boy chimed in.

'Tell me, child, why do you call your grandfather "Apu"?'

'My mamá says when I was little, I couldn't say "Abuelo".'

The old man nodded. 'It's true,' he said. 'It was as close as he could get, and it has stuck. My other grandchildren all managed to call their grandparents Abuelo and Abuela, but not this one. I have always been Apu, and his grandmother was Apa.'

'And your wife?'

'I lost her four years ago.' Alberto sighed, surprised the pain still stabbed when he had to admit she was gone.

'I'm sorry. But at least you have this little one with you.'

The old man looked at the boy and smiled at him.

'Oh, Alberto,' said Isabel, 'it broke my heart to see you poor little things. I wasn't allowed to spend time with any of you; Señora Peña saw to that. But I always kept an eye on you in particular — just to make sure you didn't get ill, or in fights.'

Isabel turned to Tino. 'Your grandfather was a very good little boy. He never complained; he worked hard and rarely got into trouble.'

Tino smiled proudly at his apu.

'Señora Peña — I remember her!' chuckled Alberto. 'It always seemed that the thinner we became, the fatter she got!'

'Oh, that woman!' said Isabel, shaking her head. 'And those priests. Always so cruel. I often chastise myself that I didn't stand up for you children. As if you hadn't been through enough.'

This time it was Alberto who laid his hand on hers. 'It was your cooking that kept us all going,' he said.

Isabel smiled, wiped her eyes with the back of her hand and put her glasses on again.

'Alberto, I'm so glad you visited.'

'So am I.'

For a while, they chatted easily. Isabel spoke of other

children she recalled with fondness. Alberto explained
they had met the man who had taken over the orphanage
and Isabel said she recollected an unpleasant general
had once visited the building as they were cleaning it for
his arrival.

Eventually, Andrés appeared and asked if they'd like
anything else. A coffee perhaps?

'Thank you, but no,' said Alberto.

Andrés nodded and smiled at his mother.

'I think it's time to continue our search,' said
Alberto to Isabel. Then, turning to the boy, he said,
'Would you like to visit the church?'

His grandson nodded excitedly.

Alberto reached into his pocket.

'Oh no,' said Isabel, raising her hand. 'Los Niños
couldn't accept your money, Alberto. And if you will
come back later, I'd be delighted to cook for you once
more.'

Chapter Eight

As I press myself behind the back of a giant barrel, I can smell the delicious old oak. Wedging my body between the cask and the stone wall, I smile. The boys will never think of looking for me here.

I fold my skirt into my lap so they won't see it as they pass. Néstor is useless at most games, including hide-and-seek, but Alberto might just spot me if I don't hide well.

I try to hold my breath, but I'm still panting from running through the cellars, so I concentrate on breathing as quietly as I can.

Papá would probably be annoyed if he knew I was hiding here. He doesn't like us playing in the cellars. He likes the stone caverns to be quiet and serene. 'Let the wine age in peace,' he tells us. But I like being down here in the cool. And I like being around the wine.

Papá often explains to us how the wine is made. He makes a story out of it. My favourite bit is the journey of a little grape. Papá talks about how it needs to be nurtured while it grows on the vine. He tells us how only the best care will make sure the grape has the right flavours to make a fine vintage. When the grape is fully grown, then it allows itself to be picked and turned into wine.

Néstor is always bored by Papá's stories, but I love them. Papá tells Néstor to pay attention because one day the vineyard will be his, but Néstor isn't interested. Last week, Alberto's papá told my papá that he should pass the vineyard on to me because I have a natural feel for it. But Papá just laughed. Later, he told Mamá, and she laughed too as if it were the funniest joke they'd ever heard.

Mamá said that for such a clever man, Alberto's papá has some crazy ideas. I felt bad for Alberto's papá. I know he was doing a nice thing for me. And I know Alberto tells his papá how mean Néstor is to me. Mamá and Papá don't believe me when I tell them he punches and pinches me. They say not to tell tales, and my brother and I should play nicely.

They would be pleased with me now. The three of us have been playing together all afternoon. We know that soon we'll be back at school, so we're playing while we can.

I shift my position a tiny bit. It's uncomfortable behind this barrel, but I know the moment I move, one of the boys will appear and find me.

In the gloomy light, I look at my fingers. My nails are dirty again. Mamá despairs of me ever becoming a lady.

I stick a finger in my mouth and work the grime out with my tooth. Then I suck the ball of dirt onto my tongue and stick it out, picking the grit up with my fingertip. I wipe my hand on the back of the barrel and move on to the next finger.

By the time I've finished all ten nails, I have a metallic taste in my mouth, and I'm very bored. Where are the boys?

Stiff and achy, I shift again, but this time I lose my balance. To steady myself, I plant my foot heavily on the floor under the edge of the barrel. I hear a splash and look down with dismay.

There is a puddle of red wine under the cask. One of my white socks is soaked with wine, and as I step into the light, I see red splatters all over the yellow skirt of my dress. Mamá is going to be furious.

Just then, I hear steps running towards me. For a moment, I consider squirming back into my hiding place, but dismiss the thought. I have bigger worries now.

'Ha! I found you!' screeches Néstor as he runs up to me.

I ignore him and try to wipe the wine off my skirt. After all the wine I've got on my clothes over the years, I know it is useless, but I have to try.

'Ha, ha, ha, ha!' my brother screams. He points a fat finger at my skirt.

'Mamá's going to be so angry with you!' he shouts, glorying in his victory.

I will him to shut up. The last thing I want is a fight with him. But Néstor just sneers at me, his chubby face glowing with delight.

Another set of footsteps run towards us. Alberto has heard Néstor's shouting. As I look up, he stops beside my brother. He stares at my dress.

'Oh, Mimi,' he says in a quiet voice.

I know he understands how I am feeling. I am always spilling things and have ruined so many of my clothes. Mamá despairs of me and now I've done it again.

Néstor is sniggering at me and pointing.

'Let's go to Chita,' says Alberto.

Yes, of course. Chita will help. She'll be busy preparing the evening meal right now, but I'm sure she'll do what she can.

As I walk past my brother, he snorts, 'I'm going to tell Mamá.'

'Don't be mean, Néstor,' says Alberto.

'You can't tell me what to do,' says my brother angrily.

Ignoring him, Alberto turns and walks along the length of the cellar with me.

I know Néstor well enough to know he feels humiliated and is fuming. Alberto is only a little older than him, but Néstor is such a baby it's as if the age difference is huge. I've heard Chita say Néstor is spoilt and our parents indulge him too much. If it were up to her, she says, she'd give him a good spanking.

Wishing it *were* up to Chita, I reach the cellar

entrance, Alberto by my side. The wine has seeped into my shoe now and the leather squelches as I walk.

Together, we climb the stone stairs and out into the shady courtyard. The sun is shining through the flowering jacaranda trees above, and the ground is covered in spots of light and purple petals.

Crossing the courtyard, we watch out for any of the workers, but they're all in the fields tending the vines. Papá will probably be out with them, and Mamá will be working at her desk. Since Papá's accountant had to join the army, Mamá has been doing the paperwork. Papá says she's very good with figures, and he hopes I've inherited her mental agility.

Mamá sometimes complains about how things have changed since the war began. Chita can no longer make many of the family's favourite dishes, and Mamá says she feels ill with worry that the *Rojos* will make the vineyard into a *collectivo*. Papá tells her it won't happen and our area is safe from the Republicans.

Alberto's papá sometimes says perhaps it would be a good thing to let the workers have some of the profit from the wine they help make. But Papá says there's not much profit these days, and anyway, he didn't put his whole life into this vineyard just to hand it over to a bunch of scallywags in berets.

Papá always finishes the discussion by telling Alberto's papá he respects their friendship too much to discuss politics. I think it's Papá's way of telling Alberto's papá to keep his opinions to himself.

Alberto's papá works for my papá, but they are also very good friends. He and Alberto eat with us, and they live in an annexe attached to the house. Alberto's papá is a chemist. He measures the levels in the wine, right from when it's just grape juice to when it's very old. He makes sure the wine isn't too high in alcohol or tannins. I don't really understand what he does, but Papá says he's lucky to have such a clever scientist working with his grapes.

These days, Alberto's papá helps in the fields, too. So many men have left to fight that most of the workers in the fields are women. At harvest time, we all go to pick grapes. The neighbours come round too, and Mamá and Chita make as much food as they can for everyone to say thank you.

As we walk across the courtyard to the kitchen, I can smell something frying. For an instant, I forget about my dress and imagine what might be for dinner. Perhaps padrón peppers, or butterbean stew.

Suddenly, there's a shout. 'Hey!'

Alberto and I turn to see Néstor standing at the top of the cellar stairs. He has an ugly sneer on his face.

'You can't tell me what to do!' he shouts at Alberto.

'Be quiet, Néstor,' I hiss at him.

Néstor ignores me and stares at Alberto.

'I'm not. I just think you should be nicer to your sister,' says Alberto.

Although we are the best of friends, I know that Alberto wishes he has brothers and sisters. His mother died when he was a baby, and his papá has never re-married.

'She's just a stupid girl,' Néstor scoffs, walking towards us.

I think my brother wishes Alberto was his friend, and he's jealous of my friendship with him.

'Don't call her stupid,' says Alberto. He sounds a bit angry now.

'I can call her what I want,' he says. 'It's you that should be careful. You're not a member of this family. You shouldn't even be playing with us. You should be playing with the workers' children.'

'Néstor!' I shout. 'How dare you speak to Alberto like that? You know that Papá and Alberto's papá are friends. Now just stop all this and grow up.'

I am a year and a half older than Néstor, and I know the one way to drive him crazy is to tell him to grow up.

He turns to me, and his small eyes flash with anger. All of a sudden, he steps towards me and, with his sizeable weight behind him, shoves me hard.

My foot turns and I fall. As I hit the ground, I hear the sound of my sleeve ripping. This is becoming the most awful day I can remember.

Néstor hears the noise too and he begins to laugh.

Then, suddenly, Alberto rushes towards my brother and throws a punch at him. It hits him in the face and Néstor falls heavily backwards, holding his nose.

Alberto turns to me. 'Are you all right?' he asks.

I nod, but I'm worried. Papá will not be happy about Alberto hitting Néstor, no matter how good friends he is with Alberto's papá.

He realizes what I'm thinking and says, 'I'll talk to my papá.'

'He's not your papá!' screams Néstor.

Alberto and I both turn to him. Like me, Néstor's still sitting on the courtyard ground. His nose is bleeding and blood drips onto his shirt.

'Just ignore him,' I tell Alberto. I have a horrible feeling in my stomach — as if something is about to happen that will change everything.

'What are you talking about?' asks Alberto. He obviously does not share my fear.

'I heard Mamá and Papá talking one night,' says Néstor quietly.

'Néstor, I'm going to tell Papá you've been eavesdropping again.'

He ignores me and carries on. 'They were talking about how when your papá married your mama, she was already expecting you.'

'That's not true,' says Alberto, but there's a tiny note of uncertainty in his voice.

'Your mamá was expecting you, but the man she married wasn't your real father.'

'Shut up, Néstor!' I shout as loud as I can, hoping to drown out what I know is coming.

'You're a bastard,' says my brother. A nasty smile breaks out on his face.

Alberto stands looking at him. He shakes his head. 'You're a liar,' he says.

Néstor starts to laugh a screeching, spiteful laugh.

'Take it back,' says Alberto loudly, but Néstor is still laughing.

I hear footsteps coming towards us, but I can't break my stare from what's happening in front of me.

'Take it back!' yells Alberto. He runs towards Néstor and throws himself on top of him, punching and kicking him with all the strength he can muster.

At that moment, Mamá appears from the entrance to the house and Alberto's papá appears at the courtyard's exit. They arrive in time to see Alberto viciously hitting Néstor, and they both run over.

'Alberto!' shouts Alberto's papá. He pulls Alberto away, and he clearly can't quite believe what he just saw. 'What were you doing?' he asks crossly. Then he sees that Alberto has tears running down his face. He can't look at his papá, staring instead at his boots.

Mamá kneels next to Néstor, fussing over him. She wipes the blood from his face with her handkerchief, asking why Alberto was hitting him. But, for once, my brother remains silent, his mouth tightly set.

By now, Chita has heard the commotion and runs into the courtyard. Seeing the boys are being attended to, she heads over to me and helps me to my feet.

'What happened, *chica*?' she asks, beginning to brush the dust off me. She hasn't noticed the wine stains. I follow the boys' lead and do not say anything. I don't think I could say it out loud – not when Alberto's papá is so close.

Alberto's papá is bending over Alberto with his hands gripping the tops of Alberto's arms. He's looking directly into Alberto's face, but Alberto doesn't even glance up.

Then Alberto's papá turns and walks towards the house. I don't know what this means. Is he now refusing to talk to Alberto? What's going to happen next?

He disappears into the dark of the house, but when he returns, he is rolling down his shirtsleeves and putting on his jacket. He carries Alberto's jacket and hands it to him.

Alberto takes the coat without saying anything. Alberto's papá turns to Mamá and says, 'Please accept my apologies for Alberto's behaviour. He and I are going to take a little drive to discuss what's just happened.'

Mamá nods and looks at Alberto. I thought she would be angry with him, but she doesn't seem to be. Instead, she appears concerned.

With his hands on Alberto's shoulders, Alberto's papá leads him past Chita and me. I stare at Alberto's face, but he doesn't look up – not even for a moment.

Their steps become quieter; then I hear the car doors slam and the engine roars to life. I watch as the old black car chugs past the courtyard, leaving a small cloud of dust behind it.

Waking up, I squint at the light shining through a crack in the shutters. I am mid-stretch when I remember what happened yesterday. I throw back the bedclothes and leap out of bed. In my nightdress and barefoot, I run down the stairs and through the house to the kitchen.

There, sitting at the table, are Mamá and Papá. Chita is at the stove, cooking eggs. No one is speaking as I burst into the warm room.

'Well?' I plead.

Mamá shakes her head.

Alberto and his papá are still not back. When they left last night, we thought they would go for a short drive. Maybe to the river, where Alberto's papá sometimes takes us all fishing.

Chita had postponed dinner, but it became so late Mamá said we would eat and Chita could put theirs aside. After grace, I could only manage a few mouthfuls, and Néstor just pushed his food around his plate. Even Mamá seemed to struggle. Only Papá had eaten well, complimenting Chita on her excellent stew.

After dinner, Mamá had suggested Néstor and I go to bed early, and for the first time ever, we agreed. I had gone to sleep straining to hear the sound of the old engine complaining as Alberto's papá drove it up the drive.

Papá looks at me and sees the tears starting to well

in my eyes. He pushes his chair back and nods to me. I climb onto his lap and push my face into his chest, feeling the bristly hair through his white shirt.

'Don't worry, Mimi,' he says softly. 'I'm sure it's just that that old car has broken down. I don't know how Raúl has kept it going so long, but it can't go on forever.'

I look at Mamá and she nods reassuringly at me.

Only Chita does not seem to agree, as she bangs and clatters far more than is necessary to cook eggs.

Mamá asks very softly, 'Mimi, sweetheart, can you tell us what happened yesterday? Why were Alberto and Néstor fighting?'

I don't know what to say, so I burrow my face into Papá's chest.

Mamá perseveres. 'Your brother won't get out of bed today. He says he's not well, but apart from a black eye, I can't see anything wrong with him. Won't you tell us what happened, Mimi?'

I think about the question, but I don't know what to say. I'm too confused. And right now, I'm too worried about where my friend is.

Papá says to Mamá, 'I'm sure it was nothing.' Then he kisses the top of my head and says, 'How about some of Chita's delicious eggs?'

I drag the long stick along the dusty earth, leaving a lined furrow. Leaning over, I take a close look at the vine I'm standing beside. Gnarled and cracked and charcoal grey, it looks ancient. Papá says Noah planted the first vine when he got off the ark. Looking at this vine, I can believe it.

The workers are all having a siesta. It's a hot, dry day and usually I would be in the cool of the house. But I want to be out in the vineyard, waiting for Alberto to come back.

In the distance, I hear a buzzing, like a loud mosquito. Lifting my hand to my eyes, I turn towards the noise. There, at the end of the drive, is a motorcycle.

I drop the stick and start running towards the house. As I run, I keep glancing over to the motorcycle, which is now near the house entrance. There is no question in my mind that it brings news of Alberto.

As I get closer to the house, I see a soldier climb off the bike and walk towards the courtyard. I can just hear him calling for Papá.

Suddenly, I don't want to run anymore. I slow to a walk, putting my hands on my hips and puffing loudly. By the time I reach the entrance to the courtyard, I am dragging my heels. I realize I don't want to know the news.

I stop by the arch, leaning in to see. Mamá and Papá are standing together at the door to the house. The soldier has his back to me, speaking to them. I can't hear what he is saying, but as I watch, Mamá puts her hand over her mouth, and Papá puts his arm around her.

They both look shocked, but Papá seems to be asking the soldier questions. The soldier shakes his head. Papá speaks again, this time more insistent. The soldier reaches into his uniform and pulls out some papers. He hands them to Papá, who looks at them carefully. He shows them to Mamá, and I see her start to cry.

Papá puts the papers into the top pocket of his shirt. He seems to be thanking the soldier, who nods to him and turns on his heel. He walks out of the courtyard, passing me without a glance. I hear him kick-start his motorbike. It takes a few attempts before he gets it going, but then I hear it driving away, its engine sounding like a mosquito again, buzzing into the distance.

Mamá and Papá have seen me. Papá beckons me to come to him. Reluctantly I walk towards them, kicking the jacaranda petals with my shoe. As I reach them, Papá hunches down to look me in the eyes.

'Darling Mimi. It's very bad news.'

I nod to let him know I want him to continue, despite the fact that my stomach is lurching.

'Alberto and his papá were in a motor accident.'

'Is Alberto all right?' I ask, my voice sounding very far away.

'No, Mimi. He isn't.' Papá takes a deep breath. 'Alberto and his papá have both passed away.'

I hear the sound of my own breathing in my ears and it sounds incredibly loud.

Mamá leans down to me and takes my hands in hers so I look at her. There are tears running down her face, but she tries to smile at me.

'They're with Alberto's mamá now, sweetheart.'

I nod but feel as if my body is not my own. My mind

seems blank and I can think of nothing — not even my best friend.

I glance up. There at the window, pale and pinched, with a dark shadow under one eye, is Néstor.

Chapter Nine

As they stepped into the church's cool interior, Alberto immediately felt a sense of calm. There was no one around, so he took off his hat and steered the boy down the aisle, pausing only to cross himself before taking a seat on a creaking pew.

'Let's say a prayer for your papá,' said the old man in a low voice.

The little boy nodded, squeezed his eyes shut and clasped his hands together. Alberto smiled at the child's prayer. Taking a deep breath, he looked up at the altar and Christ on the cross. When María Luisa was alive, they had attended church regularly. These days, he only went when obliged by a funeral or Communion. But in the peaceful silence of this small church, he remembered how he could clear his mind and pray.

Closing his eyes, he prayed for Juan Carlos. He thought of his daughter, and her husband's mother sitting beside him in the hospital. He asked God to protect and heal them all. Then Alberto remembered Rosa had her sister with her, and Cristina was away from her husband and children.

Slowly, his joints objecting, Alberto lowered himself onto the leather stool. Dropping his head, he whispered prayers for all of his family. Inevitably, his mind wandered to María Luisa, and he prayed she was at peace. He pictured her as a young woman, her head thrown back with laughter, her arms reaching out towards him. The image gave him an ache to hold her and laugh with her again. She had always breathed such life into him, her energy infectious and indefatigable.

She had hidden her illness from him for as long as she could. When, at last, she could no longer fool him she was losing weight because of a diet, or her fatigue was due to playing with her little grandson, she had admitted she had felt unwell for over a year.

She told Alberto she knew it was serious, and when the doctor confirmed the cancer was fast-moving, and there was little that could be done, she simply nodded in agreement. Alberto had been dumbfounded, unable to comprehend what was happening to his wife and best friend.

As always, María Luisa had organized everything. She'd gathered the children to tell them, and she'd given Alberto clear instructions about her funeral and burial. He had silently accepted her directions and watched like a bystander as the children fussed over her. María Luisa had insisted she would make this as easy for everyone as she could. The whole village had remarked how courageous she was, and Alberto had agreed, but cautiously waited.

Then suddenly her energy vanished, only to be replaced by pain. María Luisa had been bewildered, not comprehending why death was reluctant to follow her plan. It was then Alberto held her hand and told her he would be strong enough for both of them. Looking deep into his eyes, her fear had slowly subsided and eventually she nodded.

From then on, Alberto took control. He announced that with the help of Rosa, he would nurse María Luisa at home. Friends in the village insisted that hospital was best, that caring for a sick woman was no job for a man, but Alberto brushed the comments aside, not interested in anyone else's opinion.

Doctor Herrera had known the family for most of his life and had even delivered Rosa. He supported Alberto in his decision and helped when he could, administering pain relief and sending a nurse to show them how to care for María Luisa as her health deteriorated.

Juan Carlos coordinated the rest of the family – who would visit and when. Cristina came as often as she could, sleeping on a camp bed at Rosa's house.

Soon María Luisa became bedbound, and while her daughters bathed her and changed the bedding in the mornings, Alberto would leave María Luisa and walk out to the land. There, he would tend his small vegetable patch, bringing back what he could for the girls to add to their mother's broth.

In the afternoons, Alberto would sit on María Luisa's

bed and talk to her. Holding her hand and speaking softly, he told her who he'd seen in the village and who had sent their best wishes. He talked to her about how the plants and trees were doing on the land, and how large the lemons were growing. He described the colour of the sky and the heat in the sun, how noisy the road was and how fresh the mimosa smelt. María Luisa would listen and occasionally nod, whisper a question or smile.

His daughters were bemused. Their father had always been a man of few words, and yet now, when words were needed, he found them.

Sometimes Alberto picked wild flowers and put them in a small vase by the open bedroom window. María Luisa would look at the flowers, the delicate petals fluttering gently in the breeze.

Once, he watched her gaze rise above the flowers and up to the sky. The two of them had spent so much of their lives outdoors, he instantly understood her desire to feel the sun on her face again. With the doctor's approval, Rosa carefully wrapped María Luisa in her bedjacket and a soft blanket. Alberto and Juan Carlos then gently carried her down the stairs to where Rosa's brother, Jaime, was waiting in his car. They sat her on the back seat, padded with extra cushions.

Alberto climbed in with her, and with one arm around her bony frame, he asked his son to drive. Slowly, the car crept out of the village and onto the main road. It travelled through the countryside at a snail's pace. María Luisa saw the rows of orange trees and the old white finca, with shocking-pink bougainvillea draped over its front arches. She saw the water gushing down the irrigation channel by the side of the road and spotted a tabby lazing on a stone wall, its tail twitching. Alberto had watched her gaunt face relax as she shut her eyes. Her mouth hadn't moved, but Alberto had seen the smile in her eyes before she closed them.

When they reached Alberto's plot of land, Jaime had parked the car so that his mother could see out towards the terraces. On the nearest edge of the terrace, Cristina, her husband and Jaime's wife stood by a folding table covered with food. Five of María Luisa's grandchildren had been playing chase on the terraces, clambering up the stone walls and racing round the almond trees.

Alberto climbed out of Jaime's car, opened the door by his wife and made her comfortable with the cushions. Juan Carlos's battered old car pulled up, Tino flinging open the door to run to the game. Rosa joined the women, carrying folding chairs, which they set up so they could sit by María Luisa.

With a roar, Juan Carlos rushed towards the children, chasing the little ones, who ran away squealing with laughter. The other two fathers had quickly been dragged into the game too, and as they poured the wine, the wives laughed at their husbands getting dirty and breathless.

Alberto sat by María Luisa, holding her hand and talking quietly to her all afternoon. At times she slept, but mostly she sat, listening to Alberto and watching her family with shining eyes as they chattered and ate, played and laughed.

María Luisa had died three days later.

Rubbing his eyes with his thumb and forefinger, Alberto eased himself back onto the pew. It was only then he noticed the boy wasn't there. Glancing around the church, he couldn't see him anywhere. Panic rising in his chest, he stepped out into the aisle and started walking towards the altar.

It was then that he saw Tino standing in the gloom by a side door. The child was reaching up for the old metal handle when the door swung open with a clang. The boy jumped back and Alberto stepped quickly over to him.

Strong sunlight flooded into the church, making the child and his grandfather squint at the figure at the door.

'Hello!' said a cheery voice.

As his eyes adjusted to the light, Alberto saw a young priest dressed in a black shirt and trousers, his clerical collar pristine white.

'Good afternoon,' he replied gruffly.

'Hello,' said Tino.

The priest smiled at them both, leaving the door open and letting in the warm air.

'Were you looking for me?'

'Yes, we were,' said Alberto.

'Well, why don't we step outside? It's such a lovely day,' the young priest said.

Alberto nodded and led the boy out through the

door and into a small cemetery surrounded by a stone wall. At the back of the church stood a large carob tree, pods hanging from its wide branches. Alberto looked around.

The priest indicated an iron bench leaning on the side of the church, half shaded by the roof. As Alberto sat down heavily, the boy said, 'Apu, can I play?'

When his grandfather nodded at him, Tino immediately ran to the carob tree, searching for the best branches to climb.

The young man sat next to Alberto and smiled brightly at him. 'How can I help you, señor?'

'Romero. Please call me Alberto, Father.'

'Welcome. My name is Father Samuel.'

'Thank you.' Alberto looked again around the small cemetery. The young man waited patiently.

'Many years ago,' started Alberto cautiously, 'when I was just a child, a priest at this church looked after me.'

'Oh, how interesting. When was that?'

'During the war.'

'Aha. Very difficult times,' replied the priest carefully.

'Yes. The priest was a good man and I wonder if you know his name.'

Father Samuel's smile faded. He glanced towards the boy, who was busy climbing the tree. He seemed deep in thought, so Alberto remained quiet.

Eventually, the priest looked at the old man seriously. When he spoke, he lowered his voice. 'I've lived here for four years, and I don't believe I've seen you here before. Can I ask how you came to meet this priest?'

Alberto nodded slowly, understanding Father Samuel's reticence.

'I was lost in the war. I don't remember how I got here, but a tall priest with spectacles took care of me for a short time. He put me on a lorry that took me to an orphanage.' Alberto hesitated, wondering whether to reveal his other memory.

'Is there something else?' asked Father Samuel.

Alberto took a breath. It was all so long ago; surely it meant nothing now. 'I have a memory of an argument, between the priest and a soldier. An officer in Franco's army.'

At this, Father Samuel nodded and took a deep breath. 'Yes, that sounds like Father Francisco.'

Alberto sighed. 'Yes. That was his name – Father Francisco. Do you know what happened to him?'

Samuel looked at Alberto seriously. 'I'm afraid it is not good news. Father Francisco was removed by the army. He was accused of being a traitor and sent to a concentration camp. The records are inconclusive, but I believe he died there.'

Alberto breathed out heavily. 'That seems hard to believe. The Church supported Franco. I was taught by priests when I was in the orphanage – they often spoke of the Catholic martyrs murdered by the Republicans.'

'Yes, that's right. The Red Terror, they called it. Even before the war, thousands of Catholic clerics were killed. There were horrific reports of atrocities — executions, castrations — I even read that a priest was thrown to the bulls in a bullring.'

Alberto sucked his teeth and shook his head.

'It was understandable that the Church aligned itself with the Nationalists during the war. Your Father Francisco was a rarity: he had a strong social conscience. He refused to take sides, and instead supported those who needed help the most — the poor. But that meant that he was accused of supporting the enemy.

'These days, of course, we consider ourselves a rather more charitable institution, but back then Francisco was sadly ahead of his time.'

'How do you know this about him?' asked Alberto.

Father Samuel smiled softly. He pointed towards the rows of old stone and marble stones marking graves. 'Do you see that grave there? The one with a wooden cross?'

Alberto squinted and saw the outline of a grave. At one end stood a small, weathered cross. He couldn't see clearly, but it didn't look as if there was a name on the cross. Nodding, he turned back to the priest.

'Ever since I arrived, I've always spent time out here. I know it's a little unorthodox, but I feel close to God in the sunshine. And it's always so peaceful — I get a great deal of thinking and prayer done here.

'As I walk the cemetery, I look at the names, trying to match them with the families I see every Sunday. When I came across that grave, it had no cross. It looked as if there had been one, but it had been destroyed. I looked in the church records, such as they were, but could find no reference to it. I asked some of the people I met here. The younger ones knew nothing, but a few of the elders gave me the impression they knew something but did not like to speak of it.'

Alberto nodded. 'It's understandable that people are reticent to speak of the war. So many atrocities, so many families destroyed.'

'Yes,' agreed the priest. 'And you know how everyone fell into the Pact of Forgetting — both sides agreeing it was better to look forward than risk looking back to the divides that tore this country apart.'

'What's done is done. There's no point in picking at a sore.'

'Exactly. I didn't want to push anyone, so I left it and, truth be told, I forgot. Life in a small town is busier than you might think, Alberto.

'Then, one day, I was called to administer the last rites to an elderly gentleman. He was very ill and I sat with him for a long time. When he passed, his wife — a woman of great strength — asked me to pray with her for the soul of her husband.

'When we finished, she brought a wooden box to me. She explained that for many years her husband had been a custodian to a few churches in the area. He held the keys and looked after the maintenance of the buildings. She said that when I'd asked about the unnamed grave in the churchyard, her husband told me he knew nothing about it. But in fact he did.

'He had found a body hanging from a tree — a suicide. Together, he and Francisco buried the poor soul in the unmarked grave. She said her husband always had the greatest respect for Father Francisco and his compassion. And when the army took him away, her husband was asked to collect the father's possessions and deliver them to the bishop. He did as he was asked — but didn't hand over everything: he'd come across the small wooden box and realized it contained Father Francisco's diaries. Somehow, he didn't want them falling into the bishop's hands, so hid them in his home. Later, when I asked about the grave, he instructed his wife to give me the box on his death.'

Alberto raised an eyebrow.

'In them,' continued the priest, 'he described his life here and his thoughts and beliefs. Of course, the first diary I searched for was the one explaining the occupant of the unmarked grave. It was written before the war and documented Father Francisco's arrival here at the church.

'He wrote about the death of a friend of his, explaining that his friend had killed himself here in the churchyard — he hanged himself from that tree.'

Father Samuel pointed to the carob tree that the boy was climbing. Alberto felt a slight shiver run through him.

'Because it was a suicide, a mortal sin, he buried the body at night, in an unmarked grave. That in itself was shocking — and I understand why no one had been willing to tell me about the grave when I asked. But as I read on, I discovered something even more dreadful. Father Francisco's friend had also been a priest.'

'A priest?' gasped Alberto.

The father nodded. 'Father Francisco inherited his friend's position here in the church. In his diary, he wrote of wanting to be near the spirit of his friend. But then, reading between the lines, he became comfortable here. He supported the poor and often helped farmers with the harvest. I can imagine he was not popular with the more wealthy members of the community but the majority of the congregation seemed to warm to him quickly.'

'Father, did you read anything about his time during the war?'

The priest shook his head.

'Do you still have the diaries?' asked Alberto.

'I'm afraid not,' said the father, taking a deep breath. 'When I mentioned the diaries to my bishop, he showed great interest in them. When he asked me for them to read, how could I refuse? I believed them to be — how would one put it? — on loan. But when I mentioned them again to the bishop, he said he had sent them to the Church archivists. Although I have asked for them to be returned, I'm afraid my requests have been refused.' Father Samuel shrugged. 'Such is the Church's will.'

'That's a shame,' said Alberto quietly.

'Yes,' nodded the priest. 'But, from the little I read, it seems Francisco was a good man and a priest who was loyal to his community. I'm sure you'll understand, Alberto, that when the war came and his principles were revealed, the institution of the Church did not see him as the compassionate priest he clearly was. It's very sad.'

Alberto nodded slowly, absorbing the information. Taking a deep breath, he looked up and saw the unmarked grave.

Father Samuel followed Alberto's gaze and said, 'I believe it was Father Francisco's intention to add his friend's name to the cross. It was perhaps indelicate to do so when the village was still in shock over their priest's suicide. Many would probably consider the ignobility of an unmarked grave a fitting end for such a sinner. He was probably waiting for tempers to cool. But then the war came and the strength of feeling about the Church was such that any act like that would only fuel emotions.'

Alberto nodded. 'Poor man,' he said softly, looking towards the grave. 'Do you think he'll ever have his name on his grave?'

'It is my hope. I have submitted a letter to my bishop, asking both for the man's date of birth and any necessary details, and for permission to place a headstone on the grave.'

'Good,' said Alberto.

'Unfortunately,' sighed Father Samuel, his smile slipping again, 'the wheels of the Church roll rather slowly. The bishop referred my request to a higher level. I have been waiting over a year for a reply.'

Shaking his head, Alberto looked back at the grave. 'All this time and they still can't find a way to forgive him.'

'Perhaps,' said Father Samuel quietly, 'they know what drove him to take his life.'

Alberto paused thoughtfully, then shook his head. 'If he was a friend of Father Francisco, he must have been a good man. It is God's decision to forgive, not the Church's.'

Father Samuel nodded. 'I understand, Alberto. But protocol dictates a process must be followed. I shall write to my bishop again.'

Alberto continued to look at the grave. 'Do you know the priest's name?'

'Father Antonio,' said Father Samuel softly.

As the two men regarded the grave, Tino trotted up beside them.

'What are you looking at?' he asked.

'Nothing,' said Alberto. He turned to the child. The boy was filthy. He was grey with dust, and his legs were covered in small scratches.

'Oh dear,' said Father Samuel cheerily. 'Looks like someone could do with a wash. Why don't we let your grandfather have a moment here, and I'll show you where you can get clean?'

They both looked at Alberto, who nodded at them.

Chattering to the boy, the priest led him back into the church. For a moment, Alberto closed his eyes, letting the sun warm his face, and listened to the low buzz of the town on the other side of the wall. Then, opening his eyes, he reached into his trouser pocket and brought out his old penknife.

Alberto and the boy walked into Los Niños and looked around. The restaurant was now half full, mostly with men in their work clothes drinking beer and picking at plates of tapas. Andrés, dressed in a white shirt and black trousers, bustled around the customers, filling glasses and collecting plates.

They walked to the bar and Alberto helped the boy onto one of the high stools. The child kicked his feet side to side as Alberto wearily perched on the edge of his.

'Señores,' said Andrés, slipping behind the bar. 'Welcome back. What can I bring you?'

Alberto asked for a beer for himself and a lemon drink for the boy. When Andrés brought them, Alberto took mouthfuls of the cold beer, reflecting on what he'd heard at the church. The boy crunched his way through a plateful of crisps Andrés had placed in front of him and watched a television that hung from the ceiling at the end of the bar.

Just as Alberto was finishing his beer, the bead curtain rustled and Isabel stepped out of the kitchen.

'Doña Isabel!' said the boy brightly.

'Hello, child,' smiled Isabel. 'Hello, Alberto.'

'Hello,' replied the old man warmly. 'It's good to see you again.'

'So,' said Isabel to Tino as she leant against the side of the bar. 'What have you learnt? Are you any closer to knowing more about your grandpapá's history?'

The child suddenly looked at his grandfather. He had been distracted by the tree and had forgotten the reason for visiting the church.

Alberto nodded at the boy. He was pleased that the child had been able to play for a while.

'I found out the name of the priest who looked after me,' he said as cheerfully as he could.

'What was it, Apu?'

'Father Francisco.'

'Did you find out what happened to him?' asked Isabel.

'He was considered a traitor by the Nationalists,' said Alberto. 'It seems he died during the war.'

'Oh,' said the boy.

Isabel shook her head sadly.

'So we have reached the end of our search,' said Alberto.

'What?' said the boy anxiously.

Alberto frowned. He had expected Tino to be disappointed, but the fretful reaction surprised him.

'Well, there's no more information to be gained from the orphanage, and Doña Isabel has very kindly helped us with everything she could. Now we know about my time here in this village, before the orphanage. But there's nothing else. I don't remember anything before Father Francisco, and we've run out of clues.'

'But can't we ask someone else?' The child seemed agitated.

'Who?'

'Other old people in the town?'

Alberto and Isabel chuckled.

'What will we ask them?' said Alberto gently. '"Excuse me. Do you remember a boy who was in this village for a short time in the 1930s?"'

The boy shook his head in alarm. 'But, Apu, it can't be over already.'

'I know — it's sad we didn't get more answers. But we tried, didn't we?'

'But we didn't find your birthday, Apu!' the little boy whined, almost in tears.

Alberto glanced up at Isabel. She looked at him quizzically.

'That's what we are looking for — my birthday.'

'Ah,' said Isabel, looking at Tino. 'I understand. Birthdays are so important to a child.'

'For some reason, it has become important to me too,' said Alberto quietly.

Isabel nodded kindly.

Suddenly, the little boy burst into tears.

Chapter Ten

DANTE
24 May 1934

It's a mistake to come into the kitchen, but the smell is too tempting to resist — a wonderful mixture of frying onions and roasting meat. But one look at my wife directing the dozen or so women and girls, and the military-style manoeuvres involved in the preparation of so many dishes, and I know this is no place for a man.

The large oak table is the centre of activity, with herbs being chopped, fruit being peeled and sausages being sliced. At the far end, away from the oven, Néstor sits in a chair propped up by cushions. With chubby fingers he reaches into a bowl of shelled peas and does his best to put them in his mouth. Beside him stands Mimi, peering over the edge of the table watching Chita gutting fish. The poor girl looks too terrified to move as women work around her, brushing her with their skirts.

'Don Dante!' calls Chita with a smile. 'Have you come to help us?'

My wife turns to me, her face flushed and her usually perfect hair tousled. She tries to smile at me, but I can see she doesn't have the time for unexpected visitors.

'Chita, my wife obviously has everything under control.' I smile at the working women and add, 'The cooking smells magnificent, ladies.' Then, turning to my wife, I say, 'Perhaps I should liberate these two?' and point to the children. With relief she smiles at me and nods.

As I pick Néstor up out of his chair and take Mimi's little hand, my wife steps over to me, wiping her hands on her apron. 'Thank you, dear husband,' she says. She gives me a kiss on the cheek.

'Don't overtire yourself,' I say quietly to her. 'It's a party. I want you to enjoy it too.'

'I'll enjoy it when all the work is done,' she says. She picks up a couple of slices of chorizo from the table beside her. Popping them in my mouth, she smiles and turns back to the stove to stir a bubbling pot.

Chewing the rich, spicy sausage, I lead Mimi out of the kitchen and into the courtyard. There, some of the men are setting up tables and bringing chairs out of the house.

Raúl is kneeling on the floor, attaching lanterns to a wire for hanging. Alberto is sitting beside him watching. As we approach, I look at Mimi and see her face light up at the sight of her friend. Néstor seems unaffected and sucks on his fingers.

'Can we help?' I ask.

'Dante! Excellent timing. I'm ready to hang these lanterns. Could you take the other end?'

I set Néstor down on the floor beside Alberto, and Mimi flops down alongside them both. They watch as Raúl and I fetch chairs and climb them to carefully attach the wire onto hooks so the lanterns swing over the long tables.

When we've finished, we step back and take a look.

'It's going to be a great party, Dante,' says Raúl. He smiles sadly at me.

I put my hand on his shoulder. 'It's a celebration,' I say softly.

He nods.

I know he must feel strange about today. After many years of hard work on both our parts, Quintero's Winery has produced its first brandy. But the brandy is a memorial to the wife that he has lost.

When Angelita died all those years ago, I wanted to do something that would express the grief we each felt. I had been thinking about expanding my vintage into brandy, and it had seemed a fitting memorial. A beautiful woman of such charm and spirit deserved to be remembered forever, and the first bottle of our new brandy would do so.

The financial outlay to start producing a brandy has cost me a great deal, but now that my wine is the preferred choice of some of the most influential families in the region, the investment seems a good one.

Over the years, Raúl and I have visited other brandy- and sherry-makers around the country. In learning the process, we've inspected the barrels where the wine is aged and followed the ancient instructions for blending.

As a scientist, Raúl has enjoyed the study of the production process. And importantly, I think the project has served him well in overcoming his grief at the death of his wife. For me, it's the history. The process that has been used in Spain for centuries has a slow, methodical procedure that will continue into the future. It appeals to my sense of heritage.

Since I commissioned the building of a series of ageing barrels four years ago, we've been following the process of tapping the oldest barrel and refilling it with wine from the next oldest. As we repeat and repeat, the blending of wines over the years gives the brandy its character.

I am proud I have begun something that Néstor will carry on, and as long as the wine is good and the barrels are cared for, the brandy will only improve over the years. Even the label has been designed in the classical style with a flourish of script and the vineyard's crest.

Although our first bottle is still very young, we decided this was the perfect excuse for a celebration. It has been a difficult few years. The economic problems of the country have affected us, as they have many others, but we have done what we could for our workers and they seem content, despite the unrest around us. They also know the government is swift in arresting anyone who speaks out against land and business owners.

As my father always said, support your workers and in difficult times they will support you. So, like my father, I treat the workers as extended family. When times are difficult, I gather them and explain how we will be affected. I know many of them supported the Second Republic, with its promise of land to the workers. When nothing happened, the workers were disappointed, but they know that I am modern in my approach to their rights and their pay.

I hope the party tonight will bring us together. It's an opportunity for us to say thank you to the workers for their loyalty. They'll bring their wives and children; they'll eat well, drink too much and taste our first brandy. As Raúl says, it's going to be a great party.

'Let's take a walk,' I suggest to Raúl.

He nods to me and we turn to the children. Mimi is trying to pick up her baby brother, but he's too heavy for her, and as she half lifts, half drags him towards me, his face scrunches up and he starts to cry.

When Mimi was a baby, she rarely cried, but when she did, it was a heartbreaking sound. Maybe it's because she was our first, but often my wife and I, and even Chita, would rush to see what we could do to ease her distress.

Néstor, however, cries often and the sound is shrill and screeching. It's not an endearing noise and, I'm ashamed to say, all too often we placate him with food.

He's a portly baby, which is perhaps why he is late to start walking. But my wife insists once he's on his feet and running around, the weight will drop off him.

I lift the boy from Mimi's arms and bounce him up and down until his crying eases. He grabs my ear and pulls hard, grinning a toothy smile. His grip is strong and I have to gently prise his fingers open to release my sore ear.

'Right,' I say loudly, 'who wants to go and inspect the grapes?'

'Me!' shouts Mimi loudly and happily.

Alberto nods enthusiastically.

'Me too!' says Raúl cheerfully.

Together, the four of us stroll out of the courtyard and down to the land. The new season's growth looks good. Lines of vines with large, veined leaves stand healthy and strong. As we walk down the dusty, dry path between the crop, I stop at one vine and fold back a few of the leaves. There, hanging like a bunch of green bullets, are the grapes.

I pick one from its stalk and wipe the dust from it. Bending down, I hold it in front of Mimi and Alberto. Néstor, resting on my hip, looks over my shoulder back towards the house.

'Look, children,' I say to them both. 'What do you think this is?'

'It's a grape,' says Alberto confidently.

Grinning, Mimi shakes her head.

'It's much more than a grape, Alberto,' I say.

The young boy looks confused.

'It is the blood of Christ.'

Poor Alberto looks even more confused.

'It's the toast at a wedding,' I continue. 'It's the completion of a business deal. It's the heart that beats between family and friends. This tiny grape, children, is going to be wine. Wine that may be savoured with a loved one, or shared among many. It may be drunk as soon as it's bought, or hidden away in a cellar. But however and whenever it is drunk, in that moment, it will be a part of people's lives.

'As a family of winemakers,' I continue, 'it is our past and our future. And this grape will take a little piece of us to people we'll never meet, all over Spain. Isn't that incredible?'

Mimi nods enthusiastically. She loves to hear about the wine.

Alberto nods a little more hesitantly. Looking up at his father, he says, 'But I am not a Quintero. Papá and I are Romeros.'

Raúl gives me a worried look, but with a nod I indicate that I will explain.

'Alberto, family is not always about a name. In our case, family is more than birth. It's about an unbreakable bond of love. You and your papá have been a part of my family since before you were born, and that bond is very strong.

'And if ever you wanted proof of your role in this family, you need only look at the bottle of brandy that we will open tonight. You'll see on the label how it cele-brates you and your beloved mamá.'

The boy looks a little unsure still. I wonder how much Raúl has spoken to him about his mother. Shift-ing Néstor on my hip, I hunch down to Alberto's level.

'You are an important member of this family, Alberto. You hold a special place in our hearts. And I hope that in the future you will help Néstor run the Quintero vineyard as your father has helped me. The wine we produce today is the best we've ever made, and that's thanks to your father. It is my ancestor's name on the bottle, but there's as much of your father's soul in every sip as mine.'

I look at Raúl. He seems uncomfortable but bends his head to me in thanks. He is a good man, and I hope I tell him often enough how much I value him.

Alberto smiles at me and his soft brown eyes melt my heart – they are just like his mother's.

Ruffling his curls, I stand straight. 'Right, who can run to the fence and back the fastest?'

Before I've finished speaking, Mimi is off, running as fast as she can, kicking up tiny dust clouds behind her. Alberto gives me one last look before dashing after her.

'Thank you, Dante,' says Raúl quietly as we slowly start to walk in the direction the children are running.

'I mean every word I say.'

Raúl shakes his head and says, 'I mean thank you for taking us into your family. You knew nothing about us when we arrived and yet you took in an inexperienced chemist and his pregnant wife as if it were nothing. And now you talk about Alberto being part of Quintero's future, well, it's incredible.'

'You, Angelita and Alberto have made our lives richer,' I say gently.

'That's kind of you. But you don't know anything about us — our family, our past—'

I raise my hand to stop him. 'When you arrived, it was clear you were keen to start a new life for you and your new family. Who am I to judge your people or where you have come from? That's why I've never asked about your background . . . despite my wife's curiosity. I could see straight away that you would be good for the business and that we would get on.' I smile at him. 'And I was right, so let that be an end to it.'

After a pause, he nods.

'What do you think the brandy will taste like?' I ask him.

Raúl sighs and says, 'After four years of hard work, I just hope to God it tastes like brandy.'

There's a slight breeze and the lanterns gently sway over the bowed heads at the table. Father Sebastián is saying grace and I take a sneaky glance at my family, friends and workers.

Mimi, sitting beside me, opens one eye and squints at me. I wink at her and she shuts both eyes tight again. I, too, drop my head and listen to the father. He gives thanks to God for the strength to work the fields, for the sunshine that the grapes thrive on, for the love of the people around the table that has helped create wine to be proud of. Finally — as the youngsters start to fidget — he blesses the feast that's laid before us.

Everyone mumbles, 'Amén'; the sound is quickly replaced by spoons in dishes and cheery talk. A few of the women stand and bring large plates of the roasted baby lamb to serve the men.

I pick up a dish of chorizo and potato, and spoon some onto Mimi's plate, then some onto mine.

Reaching across for some bread, the little girl looks around her, at the people talking and laughing. Some of the men have had a few beers before coming to dinner, so the conversation is flowing easily. There's plenty of wine, so it won't be long before the talk becomes bawdy and I'll suggest my wife takes Mimi up to bed.

But for now, she's enjoying watching and listening, and every now and again she smiles at me or Alberto, who sits opposite her. She hasn't noticed she's spilt tomato sauce down the front of her best dress. Her mother will not be pleased, but I'm sure Chita will be able to remove the stain.

My wife approaches, holding a large plate. 'I've brought you your favourite,' she says. She tilts the dish for me to see. On the plate are partridges, cut in half, surrounded by onions and covered in a sauce of cider, herbs and nutmeg. The smell is wonderful and I shut my eyes and breathe in deeply as she serves me.

As she leans over me to spoon a little more sauce on

my plate, I open my eyes and plant a huge kiss on her cheek.

'Dante!' she says loudly, half embarrassed, half amused. The men on the table near us cheer.

'Gentlemen, can there be anything better than fine wine, delicious food and beautiful women?' I say loudly.

'Add family and friends to that list, Dante,' replies Raúl, raising his glass.

'To Don Dante!' shouts one of the men, his cheeks flushed.

'Don Dante!' reply the rest of the table, raising their glasses.

I nod appreciatively at them and smile at my wife as she carries on serving the partridge.

We all eat heartily, and as the table rocks with laughter at a coarse joke, I catch myself chuckling along with them. Glancing towards Raúl, I notice he has slipped out of his seat. His plate is half finished, and as I glance around the courtyard, I see him disappear into the dark of the cellar.

Just then, my wife appears beside me with a plate of food in her hand. At last, she is able to sit and enjoy the meal she has prepared. I quickly stand and offer her my chair. As she sits, I pour her a large glass of wine – she deserves it. She thanks me and turns to Mimi, tutting at the sight of the stained dress. She cuts the child's food up for her and then turns her attention to Alberto, who has a large piece of lamb on the end of his fork, which he's biting into with great enthusiasm.

Picking up my almost empty wine glass, I take this opportunity to leave, and as I walk past the tables of people, some shout my name and raise their drinks. I salute them as I pass. Reaching the cellar entrance, I turn back and see everyone is talking loudly and laughing even more loudly. This fiesta is all I hoped it would be — and we haven't even brought out the brandy yet.

I descend into the gloomy cellar. As my eyes adjust to the light, I walk down the steps to where the large oak barrels line the walls. My shoes tapping on the stone floor, I walk past the rows of barrels looking for Raúl. I find him at the far end of the cellar.

'Raúl,' I say softly.

He turns to me and I see he has tears in his eyes.

I wait as he composes himself. I sense he wants to talk, so I let him take his time.

Eventually, he says, 'I wish she was here, Dante.'

'We all do. Tonight is a celebration of her.'

He nods. I wait for him to go on.

'She wouldn't want me to tell you, but the more you talk about how Alberto and I are part of your family, the more I feel I have to tell you the truth. The truth about why we came here. About why we had to get away.'

I wait.

Eventually, he whispers, 'Alberto . . . is not my son.'

As he looks me in the eye, I try to hide my shock. I step towards him and put a steady hand on his shoulder. 'Wait,' I say firmly.

With that, I turn to the shelves of wine. Down near

the bottom is a bottle I placed there just a few days ago. I pick it up and show Raúl the label. It is one of our first bottles of brandy. He looks surprised as I hand it to him to open.

I empty the last wine from my glass and, taking out my handkerchief, wipe it clean.

Raúl eases the cork stopper out and smells the top of the bottle. I hold the glass towards him, and we both watch as the golden liquid fills it.

Swirling the brandy as I would a wine, I look at the small crown it leaves round the glass. I inhale, deeply: I can pick up woody and floral flavours. Then, pushing my nose closer to the liquid, I inhale deeply again. It is fragrant with a fruity aroma. I look at Raúl and raise my eyebrows.

Slowly, I tilt the glass and draw the brandy into my mouth. I let it open up and sense its velvety texture. Then the magic happens. Warm and smooth, the liquid flows down my throat, leaving a full bouquet in the finish. The aftertaste is short, proving the youth of the brandy, but the flavour is good. I am pleased.

Handing the glass to Raúl, I nod with approval.

He does the same as I did, savouring the smell first, then sipping the brandy. He closes his eyes and I see his face relax.

When he opens his eyes, he smiles at me. I smile back. We've done it.

'Now,' I say gently, 'tell me.'

Raúl takes another deep breath and hands me back the glass.

'I had known Angelita most of my life. We met when we were a little older than Alberto and Mimi. I adored her. If it is possible to fall in love as a child, I did. Even as a little girl she was beautiful. That long hair and those soft brown eyes — she just grew more incredible as she got older.

'We went to separate schools, but we spent our evenings and weekends together. We would talk of everything — and I thought we would be together forever.

'On the day that I left home to go to university, she went to the station with me. It was there that I kissed her for the first time. I told her that I loved her.

'As I began my studies at university, I planned our life together — how I would become a renowned research scientist, and we would marry and have at least four children.' Smiling, Raúl sadly shakes his head. I hand him the brandy and he takes a deep drink.

'I wrote every week and at first she replied regularly. Then less so. Then barely at all.

'The next time I returned home, I visited her. I was surprised at how much she had changed. She was thin and serious — it was as though her youth and sparkle had disappeared. She was courteous but kept me at a distance.

'I spoke to her sister, Mercedes, about her. She said that Angelita had started disappearing, sometimes late at nights and she refused to speak of where she'd been.

'At first, Mercedes said Angelita had been happier than she'd ever seen her. But over a few months, the happiness had become something darker. During this time, Angelita turned to God. She started to visit church whenever she could. She barely ate, she left school and the life seemed to be seeping out of her.

'Mercedes confided in me that she believed Angelita was having an affair with a married man. She thought her sister was visiting church to repent her sins but the guilt was making her ill.

'I was shocked, appalled and distraught in equal measure. How could she change from being the innocent girl I had given my heart to, to another man's mistress?'

I shake my head and refill the glass. Raúl takes another drink.

'Eventually, I confronted her,' he continues. 'At first, she looked horrified at my accusation. I suppose she was so entrenched in it that she couldn't see what others could. Then she told me that yes, she was having an affair with a man who could never be hers. I begged her to leave him, but she said she loved him with all her heart.

'I became emotional and I'm ashamed to say I wept in front of her. She looked at me with such pity that I had to leave. I returned to university. I threw myself into my work and did well at my exams. The next time I came home, I avoided Angelita's family and her friends. But the day before my return to college, Angelita appeared at our door.

'She looked terrible, dark circles under her beautiful eyes, and her long hair was lank. She asked if I could forgive her and allow her to talk to me. Of course, I said yes to both.

'We went for a walk in the park. There, she told me that the affair was over. He had finished it a few months earlier. I expressed my relief, but she broke down in tears. She told me that she was pregnant. The father had no idea and she couldn't tell him now that they were no longer together.

'We both knew her family would disown her. She told me that no one else knew, not even Mercedes, and she had turned to me, her only true friend, to help. She said she would understand if I wanted nothing to do with her. But I took her to me and held her in my arms.

'The solution seemed obvious to me. She would marry me and we would leave the area. I would raise the child as mine, and she would never have to see the father again. She couldn't believe it – that I would be prepared to take care of her and another man's child without a second thought.

'I told her that I loved her, that the past didn't matter. If she'd have me, we would start a fresh life together.'

I smile at my friend. 'You are a good man, Raúl. A romantic fool, but a good man.'

Taking another sip of brandy, he continues, 'The rest you know. We married quickly and I began looking for work. We chose this area as neither of us had family or friends near here. Meeting you was the best thing that could have happened to us: learning about the wine business alongside having the opportunity to apply my scientific knowledge to winemaking.

'We were happy. As her pregnancy developed, Angelita grew healthy; being so far from that other man seemed to help. Very occasionally I would catch her looking out of the window and I knew she was thinking of him. But she said she loved me and that she was look-ing forward to the arrival of this baby and many others.'

Raúl takes a deep breath and pauses. Then he carries on. 'You saw what her death did to me. I wasn't sure that I would recover. But the support I found here and the unconditional love of that little baby kept me going.

'I've never said anything to Alberto about his father. I think it's enough that he has no mother. Perhaps when he's older, I'll tell him, or perhaps there will never be a need to tell him.

'Whatever happens, I see him as my son. He is his mother's son in his looks, but he has picked up certain habits and characteristics from me, too. I adore him as I adored her. I'm very lucky, Dante. When I look into his eyes, I have the chance to see my adorable Angelita every day.'

Raúl stops talking and drains the glass.

'Well, your secret is safe with me, Raúl. If you decide

to tell Alberto about his father, I will be here to support you. My wife and I are proud to be the family he doesn't have.'

'Thank you, Dante,' says Raúl. 'I've kept this secret for so many years. It is a relief to finally talk to someone about it.'

'I'm proud that you decided to confide in me, my friend,' I say, gripping his arm. 'Now, what do you say – shall we let the rabble outside try our fantastic brandy, or shall we stay down here and keep it to ourselves?'

Chapter Eleven

The boy sucked noisily on the ice lolly, occasionally licking orange drips off its end. His grandfather pulled gently on a cigarette — a rare treat he sometimes allowed himself. They sat on a cold stone bench set back from a quiet road. The leaves of a line of palm trees rustled quietly above them, and cast a little shade from the sun.

'Are you all right?' asked Alberto. When the boy had calmed down, he'd taken him out for this small treat.

The boy stopped licking the ice lolly and looked seriously at his grandfather. 'We have to find your birthday, Apu,' he said.

'It might not be possible,' replied the old man. 'Look how difficult it has become already.'

Tears welled up in the little boy's eyes again.

'Don't be upset. Even if we don't find it, I have found Isabel. I never thought I'd see her again in my lifetime. So something good has—'

'But we have to find your birthday, Apu,' interrupted the child.

'Why? Why is it so important to you?'

Tino looked down, crunching the last mouthful of his lolly and swinging his legs. Alberto waited patiently for him to speak.

'Just because,' Tino eventually said, his bottom lip protruding.

'Because what?' the old man pressed gently.

'Because of God.'

'God?'

'Mmm.'

'What does God have to do with my birthday?'

'Nothing.'

The old man waited again, confused.

After a short wait, the boy sighed loudly.

'It's just fairer, that's all. If you get your birthday back, Papá will get better.'

'What do you mean?'

'I prayed. I said to God, if I help you look for your birthday and we find it, then he'll make Papá better.'

Alberto stared at the child, bemused and touched. 'So you suggested a deal to God? If you do something nice for me, then he'll do something for you?'

The child nodded, still looking at his swinging feet.

'Well, I don't know for sure, but I don't think God does deals. If he makes your papá better, it's because he loves you, and Mamá and Papá.'

'But what if Papá doesn't get better? Does that mean God doesn't love me?'

The old man could see the tears welling up again and heard a wobble in the boy's voice. He pulled the child towards him and held him. 'God will always love you. Just like Mamá and Papá and me.'

The little boy let out a sob, and the old man held him tighter.

'Your papá is getting better — remember what Mamá said? But we must both keep praying, and telling God how much we love Papá.'

The old man sat holding the small boy for quite some time.

It was mid-afternoon, and the restaurant was emptying when they sat down to eat their meal. Alberto had accepted Isabel's invitation but told the boy they would start their journey home afterwards.

The old man was more disappointed than he had ever imagined he would be when they'd started this journey. Having had a few of his memories jogged back to life, he wanted to know more. Where had he come from? How had he arrived at this village? What of his family? There was so much to learn, but they had reached the end of their search.

Isabel sat beside him, watching in delight as Tino wolfed down the food she'd put before him. She turned to look at Alberto, who gave her a sad smile.

'I'm sorry,' she said.

'Don't be. This search has brought me to you. I'm glad to have seen you again.'

Isabel smiled back. 'I'm very glad you found me. In fact,' she said, easing herself up from the table, 'I know the perfect thing to mark the occasion.' Isabel turned and walked slowly to the bar, leaning heavily on her stick. Andrés appeared as if from nowhere to help her, but she waved him away.

Leaning behind the bar, she opened a dark wood cabinet and reached towards the back of the shelf. When she stood straight again, Alberto saw she was holding a dark green bottle. 'I save this for very special occasions,' Isabel said. She walked back towards them.

By the time she reached the table, Andrés was placing two brandy glasses beside them.

'And one for yourself, Andrés,' said Isabel.

Andrés raised an eyebrow to her, but Isabel nodded. 'If it weren't for this man, you would never have been born,' she said.

Andrés silently placed another glass on the table.

With her gnarled fingers, Isabel twisted the cork stopper out of the bottle and poured a little into each of the glasses.

'This brandy was my husband's favourite. It's changed now — it's not as good — but luckily my husband bought a case many years ago. This is the last bottle of that case. I can't think of a better person to enjoy it with, Alberto.'

As Tino looked on, Alberto nodded graciously to Isabel.

'What are we toasting, Mamá?' asked Andrés, raising his glass.

'Alberto?' asked Isabel.

The old man paused a moment, swirling the glass

and watching the rich umber liquid slide round inside. Finally, he raised his glass and waited while the others raised theirs. The boy raised his glass of pop.

'To friends. Friends we've lost and friends we've found,' said Alberto. He tilted his glass towards Isabel.

'To friends,' they all chorused.

Alberto took a large sip and let the brandy sit in his mouth, savouring its smooth flavour. Swallowing slowly, he turned the bottle to see the label.

'Apu,' said Tino excitedly, 'can I try some?'

'I don't think you'll like it, young man,' said Isabel, laughing.

'But it's a special bottle. I'd like to just try it. Can I, Apu?'

But Alberto wasn't listening. He was staring intently at the brandy bottle. As Isabel and the boy looked at him, he picked up the bottle and looked closely at the label on the front.

'Alberto?' said Isabel.

'Apu?'

Slowly, a smile spread across Alberto's face.

'Apu?' came the whisper in the dark.

'Yes,' came the gruff reply.

Alberto shifted in the bed. Andrés had insisted the pair of them should stay the night in his apartment, and his wife had made a fresh bed for Alberto and the boy.

'I told you we were going to find your birthday – and I was right!'

'We haven't found it yet. And I told you that I don't think that God does deals. You have to believe that Papá will get better. Believe it in your heart.'

'I do, Apu,' said the small voice. Then, 'When Papá is better . . .'

'Mmm?'

'Will he be . . . ?'

'What?'

'Will he be the same?'

'You heard your mamá say they were starting to remove the bandages. He is getting better.'

'No. I mean will he be the same as before?'

Alberto sighed. 'I don't know. I hope so.'

'But he was in a big explosion, Apu,' said the boy, becoming distressed.

Closing his eyes, the old man saw a blast – a burst of light and heat. But it wasn't a boiler he saw; it was a car. He frowned and the image began to fade.

'What if he can't do things anymore?' carried on the boy. 'What if he can't play football with me, or take me swimming?'

Alberto shook his head, still trying to dispel the image of a burning car and an unsettling feeling in the pit of his stomach.

'He will always be your father,' he said gently. 'Whatever happens, he will love you and care for you.'

'But he won't be the way he used to be. And the kids at school will laugh at me because there's something wrong with my papá.'

'Stop it,' said Alberto fiercely. 'I will not let you speak like that. If other children laugh, then they are not worth knowing. You will find your true friends. But this is not a time to worry about yourself. Now is the time to be brave — for your father and, more importantly, your mamá.'

In the dark, he heard the boy snuffle. He reached over and patted the boy's head.

'The doctors are very clever these days. They will do everything they can for your papá. It's not like when I was young. When I was at the orphanage, there were children who had been hurt terribly in the war.'

'Really?' came the small voice.

'Yes. Children who had been scarred or lost limbs. Many of them were younger than you and had survived all sorts of dreadful things. One boy I knew had been in a house that was hit by a shell. The house was reduced to rubble. He wasn't dug out by rescuers until the next day. All of his family were dead. They took him to hospital, and he saw injuries there that you couldn't begin to imagine.

'He was nearly completely deaf, after the noise of the explosion. He was confused and scared, so when he could, he ran away from the hospital.'

'Where did he go?'

'He found his way back to his street and some neighbours took him in. He lived with them until hunger and fear drove them to escape the city.'

'So he got away?'

'No. The Nationalists caught them. The older boys and men were shot.'

The boy gasped.

'The women were taken to prison, and the younger children were split up and taken to different orphanages. They were lucky not to have been killed too.'

'And you met him at the orphanage?'

'Yes. His hearing came back slowly, but he couldn't bear loud noises. I was quiet and he felt comfortable with me.'

'It sounds awful, Apu.'

'It was. That's why people never talk about it these days. But when you think things are difficult for you, think of what others have been through. Your troubles will seem easier then.'

There was silence while the boy seemed to contemplate his grandfather's words.

'Now,' said the old man, 'it's late. Time to sleep.'

'First, tell me again what you remembered, please, Apu.'

Alberto yawned, tired. 'It was the label on the brandy bottle. I recalled seeing it before. And when Doña Isabel showed me the wine as well, I remembered a vineyard.'

'Do you remember any people, Apu?'

'No. Just a big house with a courtyard and rows and rows of vines.'

'And the name on the bottle?'

'Quintero? I recognized that too.'

'Is it the name of the people who make the wine?'

'I suppose so.'

'Maybe they know your family, Apu!'

'Maybe. We'll find out tomorrow.'

'Apu?'

'Yes.'

'I think we're going to find your birthday tomorrow.'

Alberto was silent. It had surprised him how much his mood had changed this afternoon: from the disappointment of reaching a dead end to the excitement of finding a new clue. In the bar just before they went to bed, they made plans to visit Quintero's Winery the next day. The address was on the label, and although Alberto had never been to that area as an adult, everything about it seemed familiar.

And yet in the pit of his stomach lay an unsettling feeling — a very mild fear. Perhaps he would not like what he found. Perhaps questions would be answered only with questions. And now all these memories from his time at the orphanage were flooding back too, the war seemed closer. He couldn't remember a time since he'd lost María Luisa that he'd felt such extreme emotions.

But the boy was right. It felt as if answers were within his reach. His family, his birthplace, his birthday: it seemed likely that if they discovered one, the others would follow.

He wondered if his father had been a worker at the vineyard. He knew many vineyards had become collectives during the war. Many wine producers had gone out of business, but as the bottles in Isabel's cabinet proved, Quintero's had not.

He heard the child's breathing become deeper and knew that he was asleep.

Quintero. He had always been sure his name was Romero. Isabel had reminded him of the paper in his pocket that spelt out his name. She had said there was writing on the other side. It was in another language she recalled – German or English, she thought.

He had a vague recollection of a soldier writing the name down, but it was muddled. Soldiers and Father Francisco; the faces and uniforms were unclear to him. But the name – Alberto Romero – had always seemed right.

Yet now he wasn't quite sure. There was something about the name Quintero that gave him a sense of belonging.

Alberto lay in the dark trying to grasp the memory, but it was nothing more than a wisp.

The rhythm of the clapping and the strumming of the guitar reminded Alberto of evenings on the farms he'd worked on as a young man. As the taxi roared down the empty road, the driver tapped his thumbs on the steering wheel in time to the traditional music that echoed around the car.

On the horizon, blue mountains merged into the distant grey clouds. All around them, the undulating land bore line after line of dark green vines. There were no people in the fields, although, far in the distance, Alberto could see a bright red tractor lumbering slowly along.

Alberto looked at the sleeping boy, whose chin was wedged firmly into his chest. It had been a late night, and the whole family had been up early. Andrés had apologized for not being able to drive them to Quintero's, but he had to receive deliveries at the restaurant and he didn't want to leave all the work to his mother. Thanking him, Alberto had told him that he and his mother had done more than enough.

Isabel had come to wish them goodbye and good luck. She had given the boy a parcel of food for the journey, and the family had waved them off as they walked to the bus stop.

The bus had dropped them at the nearest village and they had found a taxi to take them out to the vineyard. They were now only a few minutes away. For the first time, Alberto had a tingle of anticipation in the pit of his stomach.

'Are you taking a tour of the vineyard, señor?' asked the driver.

'Maybe,' said Alberto. He wanted to be left alone to his thoughts.

The driver took the hint and went back to tapping along to the music. As the road gradually began to rise, Alberto saw a building in the distance. Leaning forward, he squinted at it. The driver noticed.

'Señor, that's the old hacienda. That's Quintero's.'

Alberto nodded, staring at it, realizing it meant something to him. He heard the boy stirring and turned to him.

'Apu?' said the sleepy child. He yawned and rubbed his eyes.

'We're nearly there.'

The boy joined his grandfather, looking blearily in the direction he pointed.

'Is that your old house?' he asked, wide-eyed.

'I don't know,' said Alberto quietly. He shook his head.

As they drew level with the stone building, the driver turned off the main road. A large sign proclaimed, QUINTERO'S WINERY — TOURS AND WINE TASTING AVAILABLE. The car rumbled up a wide, dusty drive, and Alberto could see a series of new low-rise buildings behind the large old house.

The taxi pulled up outside the building. Alberto paid with some coins from his small purse. The driver thanked him and gave him his number for when he was ready to be picked up.

The taxi drove off, leaving Alberto and the boy standing outside the building. A sign directed them through a large arch to the reception. Following the

arrow, they entered a cool courtyard shaded by jacaranda trees.

Alberto stopped and looked around. It was so familiar to him it was as if he'd only been here last week. The
sensation unnerved him, but a bubble of excitement
rose in his chest.

Tino looked up at him and smiled. Alberto squeezed
his hand. He owed the child a great deal.

They entered the hacienda through a large doorway.
Inside, a young woman sat at a reception desk, talking
rapidly on the phone. She was discussing the delivery of
an order to Sweden. She saw Alberto and raised a finger
at him — she would just be a minute.

Alberto gazed around. The room did not seem
familiar. Modern furniture created a waiting room,
with leaflets, brochures and wine magazines on every
table. He had the sense that the building should smell
of food, but it did not. It smelt of furniture polish.

He walked back to the open door and looked across
the courtyard. On the opposite side, a large sign that
said, CELLAR, hung over a wooden door.

Tino came up beside him and leant against his hip.

Finally, the woman finished her conversation and
turned to Alberto.

'How may I assist you, señor?' she asked.

'Good morning, señorita,' he said politely. 'Could
you tell me, are the owners here today?'

'Do you have a meeting booked?' she asked.

'No,' said Alberto. 'This is not business; it's personal.'

The woman looked at the boy, who smiled at her. She smiled back and her face softened.

'I'll see what I can do, señor. Could I have your name, please?'

'Romero.'

'Thank you, Señor Romero. Please take a seat while I call through for you.'

Alberto nodded his thanks and turned to sit in a large leather armchair. He was not used to such expensive furnishings and felt uncomfortable, but the boy followed him and clambered onto his knee.

'Apu?' he whispered.

'Yes.'

'We're nearly there.'

'Let's see.'

Alberto heard the woman talking quietly on the phone, but couldn't make out what she was saying. She seemed to be cajoling the person on the other end. Eventually, she put the phone down and smiled at Alberto.

'The owner will be down shortly. Can I get you anything? Coffee, water?'

'Thank you. No.'

The girl nodded and went back to her work behind the desk.

After a few minutes, Alberto heard steps coming

down the stairs, and when a door opened, he saw a middle-aged man approaching. The man was well dressed and clean-shaven, and his shoes clicked on the polished floor as he walked towards them.

The boy jumped off his grandfather's knee and Alberto stood.

'Señor Romero,' said the man smoothly. He offered his hand. 'My name is Javier. I am the owner.'

Alberto shook the man's hand.

'Please, señor, come up to my office,' said Javier. He directed them towards the door from which he had just come.

The old man and small boy climbed the stairs to a large office on the first floor. Windows on both sides of the room gave views over the extensive vineyard. Air-conditioning hummed quietly, and Alberto thought it sad the windows weren't open to allow a cool breeze and the scent of the plants to enter.

The man sat behind a large desk covered in computers and gadgets Alberto did not recognize. On the wall behind the desk was a selection of framed certificates. Alberto sat on an upright chair and Tino stood beside him.

'How may I be of service, Señor Romero?' asked the man when he was settled.

'Could you tell me,' began Alberto awkwardly, 'did your family run this vineyard during the time of the war?'

'My family? The war?' asked Javier, surprised. 'No, no, not at all. My family were not in the wine business at all.'

Alberto remained still.

'My father was a businessman. I took over his business and now have a number of successful businesses of my own. Three years ago, I decided to branch out into wine. I bought this winery then, and have since bought two more small ones. I'm modernizing and consolidating them.'

'Oh,' said Alberto.

'Yes,' said Javier. 'This winery was not doing well. The processes used were old-fashioned and inefficient. There was no room for growth, and they had no international connections. In just a few years, I've invested a great deal to modernize the production and now our export capacity is as good as any major wine brand you can name.'

Alberto looked out of the window. Disappointment overwhelmed him again. Tino looked at him sadly.

Javier saw their reaction and continued, 'Señor, I believe the family I bought the business from were here during the war.'

Alberto turned to him, his eyes sharp.

'In fact, I know they were. In our literature, we mention that the winery was owned by one family for nearly two centuries. That's where the name came from – the Quintero family. We considered changing it, but it's a solid name that our marketing department believed we could build on.'

Javier stood up and walked to a bureau at the back of the room.

'If it's the Quinteros you're looking for, this may be of help,' he said, opening a drawer.

Alberto stood and he and the boy crossed the room to join Javier.

Javier pulled a plastic file out of the drawer. He opened it and took out some old black-and-white photos.

'I believe this is the family,' he said. He held up one of the pictures.

Alberto and the boy looked closely. The photo was taken at the front of the house and showed a group of four people. Their clothes suggested it was the 1950s. In the centre was a large, balding man in a white shirt. He was trying to look serious, but Alberto could see his smiling eyes. Next to the man was a smart woman, and beside her, a fat teenage boy and a pretty young woman.

'This,' said Javier, pointing at the boy, 'must be Néstor. It was Néstor Quintero that I bought the winery from.'

Alberto nodded.

Javier gave Alberto the photo and shuffled through the rest of the pictures. 'That one was obviously taken after the war, and others seem to be a bit later. I'm not sure if they help you at all?'

Alberto was peering closely at the girl. The whole family seemed familiar, but the girl was particularly memorable. Turning the photo over, he was disappointed to see there were no names.

'Señor?' said Javier.

'I'm sorry. This is what we are looking for, thank you. I don't suppose you know where Don Quintero lives now?'

Javier paused for a moment.

'I'm sorry to say, señor, that Néstor Quintero died shortly after the sale was completed.'

Alberto's shoulders slumped.

'With the money from the sale, he bought a large house near the city. I remember him saying he never wanted to live on a farm again. Sadly, he had a heart attack not long after he moved to his new home.'

'That's very sad,' agreed Alberto.

'I know he had a wife and children. You could perhaps find them in the phone book?' suggested Javier.

Alberto looked at the photo again in his hand. 'Do you know anything about the girl in the photo?'

'The young woman? Yes, of course, I forgot. She is Néstor's sister. Her name is Miriam.'

'Miriam,' said Alberto, sounding the name. It didn't sound quite right.

'Now, her address we do have,' said Javier.

'You do?' asked Alberto, brightening.

'Yes. She became involved in the negotiations for the

business. Everything was in Néstor's name, and he was focused on getting the best price he could. To be honest, I would have paid more for it, but he got a fair amount of money.

'Anyway, at first Néstor said he wanted nothing — the business, the house, even the furniture would be included in the price. He said he wanted a fresh start, with nothing of his old life here.

'But, one day, Miriam contacted me direct. She said she had spoken to Néstor and had persuaded him that some items were family heirlooms. Though he wanted nothing, she wished to have something to pass on to her children.

'She mentioned a few pieces of furniture, which was fine as we were planning to modernize the rooms to create offices anyway. But then she said she wanted the collection.'

'The collection?' asked Alberto.

'The collection of wine, señor,' said Javier seriously.

'Ah.'

'Well, you can imagine my disappointment. It was a collection of all the best vintages the vineyard had ever produced. Just a few bottles from selected years. It was an incredible wall of wine down in the cellar. I had planned to make it a feature of the tours.

'In the end, the lawyers got involved. While I think Néstor was angry and just wanted to complete the sale, Miriam persuaded him not to move forward until I agreed to this condition. Through the lawyers we re-negotiated the price down.

'I respect Miriam for her decision — after so many years, it's only right that a family's history is maintained. I don't know if it's true, but I did hear that Néstor asked Miriam to pay him for what he had lost in the renegotiations. His own sister. He was not a generous man.'

Alberto nodded.

'But,' said Javier cheerfully, 'after the sale, we organized delivery of the collection to Miriam's house. And as a personal gift, for the past few years we have sent her a bottle of our best wine and brandy to add to the collection. So we have her address in our files. Would you like it?'

Alberto looked down at the photo again. The young woman was smiling and squinting in the sunshine. Her dark hair was swept up in the style of the time, but she looked natural and at home out of doors. Her dark eyes shone and Alberto knew he had to see her again.

'I would very much like to have her address, thank you.'

'No problem,' said Javier. He crossed back to his desk and picked up the phone, then spoke to the receptionist and asked her to find Miriam's address for Señor Romero.

Alberto looked down at the boy and nodded. The child grinned back at him.

'Oh, and, Señor Romero,' said Javier, putting down the receiver, 'if you wouldn't mind, perhaps you would take those photos with you? We found them when we were having some decorating done and have never got round to sending them on.'

'Of course,' said Alberto. He slid the photos into the folder and passed it to the boy. Tino slipped the folder under his arm and held it tightly.

Javier then led them down the stairs and back to reception, where the girl was picking a piece of paper up from the printer.

'Señor Romero, it was good to meet you,' said Javier. He offered a hand. It was clear he was keen to get back to his work.

'Thank you for your time,' said Alberto. He shook Javier's hand.

'I'll leave you in my receptionist's capable hands,' said Javier. He turned and disappeared through the door.

'Here you are, Señor Romero,' said the girl, offering him the piece of paper.

'Thank you,' said Alberto. He looked at the printed details. 'Do you know if this is far from here?'

'No, it's not too far. Maybe twenty minutes on the *autopista*. Would you like me to call a taxi for you?'

Alberto nodded. He was unused to taking taxis – it was an extravagance he couldn't usually justify. But this journey was special and all too soon he would be back at home. Why not enjoy the treat?

'Apu?' said the boy excitedly as the girl called the taxi company.

'Yes.'

'Do you remember Señora Miriam?'

'I believe I do.'

'Do you remember the family?'

'They seem very familiar, yes.'

'But they're not your family?'

'No. They are not my parents.'

'I wonder how you knew them.'

'Miriam will know.'

Tino jiggled with excitement.

'Señor,' said the receptionist, putting down the phone, 'the taxi will be about half an hour.'

'Thank you,' said Alberto.

'Can I offer you anything while you wait? Some coffee?'

'No, thank you,' said Alberto. 'But . . .'

'Yes?'

'No, I don't want to inconvenience you further.'

'Please, señor, I'd be happy to help.'

'I was wondering if it would be possible to see the cellar. Just for a moment?'

The receptionist smiled. 'Señor, it would give me great pleasure to give you a tour of the cellar. To be honest, I've spent all morning talking to businessmen about shipments and payments. It would be nice to smell the oak barrels and talk about the wine for a change.'

Smiling, she opened a drawer and pulled out a large bunch of keys.

'Thank you very much,' said Alberto.

'So,' said the receptionist to the little boy as she led them out into the courtyard and towards the cellar door, 'let's see what you know about how wine is made.'

Chapter Twelve

RAÚL

7 November 1932

Her long dark hair is wound in a knot at the top of her head. Her soft brown eyes look to the right, and the tiniest hint of a smile flitters around the edge of her full lips. I know that smile — she is smiling to herself at what she considers a ridiculous situation.

And sitting for a photo would have seemed ridiculous to her. She was young and full of energy and wanted to be out living life — not creating a moment for history. But I, for one, am glad that someone — probably her father — insisted that she sit for that moment.

Holding the picture up to the light, I take a sip of my wine. Again I taste the mustiness and remind myself that I must mention my concerns about the oxidization to Dante. Shaking my head, I recall the days when I could enjoy a glass of wine without performing a chemical analysis.

I turn my attention back to my little Angel. What would she want me to do? For nearly two years, I've avoided this question. There has always been a reason not to think of it.

I was barely able to function those first few months after she died. Dante and his wife had given me all the support they could, and Chita had taken the babe into her care. In fact, it was Chita, rocking baby Alberto and humming him a lullaby one evening, who had commented on his eyes — that they were just like Angelita's. Standing over her, I had looked into the baby's eyes. And I had seen my Angelita looking back at me.

That was the beginning of my recovery. With Chita's help, I learnt how to care for a baby. In the night, I was the one to go to him. It was I who made him weak camomile tea when he was teething. When he started eating, it was I who chopped long slices of pear for him to gnaw on.

Of course, I had also resumed my work for Dante and the vineyard, so my days were occupied. Dante had insisted Alberto and I join the family at mealtimes. Mimi was just a baby too, then, and Chita clucked and cooed over the two of them as Dante, his wife and I ate and talked into the evening.

Alberto was nearly nine months old when Dante had broached the subject. Mimi had been baptized as an infant. Would Alberto be baptized soon? I realized I had been deliberately pushing the thought out of my mind. I explained it was complicated; Angelita's headstrong opinions about religion meant I would need to think about it. Dante nodded and left it at that.

Shortly after, the harvest started. One of our busiest times of the year had given me an excuse to ignore the situation for a while longer. By the time things began to ease, Alberto had begun walking. The joy I took from leading him around the room gave me such delight it was all I could think about.

And so it continued: looking for and finding a reason not to think about baptizing the child. But today, after Mass, Father Sebastián sought me out and asked me directly if I would like him to prepare for Alberto's baptism.

So now there's no more procrastinating. It is time to make a decision. Taking a deep breath, I look at Angelita again. This photo, taken years before we were married, shows a young girl before the complications of life and love. If I had asked that girl if she wanted her child to be baptized, she would have laughed at me and asked why in heaven not.

But the woman I married was scarred by a broken heart and a confused relationship with religion. We were married in a small chapel with only our immediate family present. Even then, she had seemed uncomfortable and agitated during the service and, at one point, had nearly fainted. Everyone assumed it was the importance of the occasion, but I knew it was probably the pregnancy, which we hid from our families. The young priest who performed the rites was patient and caring with her and completed his duties as speedily as he could.

When we arrived at Quintero's, we were asked to join the family at church on our first Sunday. I, of course, agreed, but on the morning, Angelita said she felt ill and asked me to go without her. The following Sunday, she again refused to go. By then, I knew it was not illness that was keeping her away.

One evening as we lay in bed together, my hand resting on her growing belly, I asked her why she refused to go to church. In the darkness, she tried to explain. Once, she had believed unconditionally, she said. Truth be told, at that time she didn't think about it — she recited the words and prayed for childish things. Then she had found herself in a situation where she had needed God. Only He had the answers she was searching for. But God, who had it within His capacity to help her and make her joyous, had taken away her dreams of happiness. In her mind, He was a spiteful and vengeful God and she would not turn for help from Him again.

Since our engagement, we had never spoken about her affair, but I could see that was where God had disappointed her. She must have asked for God to find a way for this married man and her to be together. But instead her lover had broken off the affair. Unable to blame the man she loved, she blamed God instead.

I had gently suggested that over time she might see that perhaps the Lord really did have her best interests in mind. After all, He had brought us together. At this, she had remained silent but pulled my arm around her.

I held her tightly and silently thanked God for bringing her back to me.

Over the months, however, she continued to stay away from church. I worried it might affect our relationship with the Quintero family, but Dante and his wife had fallen in love with my Angelita too, and it seemed we would all forgive her anything.

We never spoke of religion again. I never asked her if she wanted her baby baptized. But in my heart, I knew what her answer would have been.

The hypnotic sound of the cicadas reverberates along the river's edge. The afternoon sun is warm, and the air is still. I can smell the faint fragrance of oleander, and, high above, the ash trees gently rustle their leaves.

I check my rod again, but there's no interest from the fish. They're having a lazy Sunday afternoon too. This is my favourite spot for fishing. At least, I make a show of fishing. In fact, I rarely catch anything, much to Chita's amusement.

The truth is, this is my favourite spot for thinking. I found it not long after Angelita's death. Even after two years, I find anywhere near the vineyard has some memory of her. In our home, the small annexe on the edge of the hacienda, I relish the sense of her in every room. Out in the vineyard, I can see her strolling easily down the dusty lines between the vines. On visits to the town, I catch a glimpse of her laughing with the old men sitting on the fountain's edge, or in the market pressing a melon to test its ripeness.

Most of the time, I enjoy the reassurance that she once existed in this place and in all our lives. But early on, there were times when the grief was so intense I wanted to be somewhere she had never been. One day, a few months after her death, I climbed into the car and drove, somehow stumbling across an old track that brought me down to the river. At once, I'd felt at peace. The pain seemed less raw as I listened to the water and felt its fresh air on my face.

When I mentioned the river to Dante, he told me he and his friends had spent many happy afternoons fishing further upstream — it seems the river is full of catfish, and in his day they had caught some big ones. When I saw his enthusiasm, I'd been worried he would want to join me. But he'd found his old fishing rod and given it to me with a smile and some handy tips.

As I sit, my arms resting on my raised knees, I look to the other side of the river. An ancient wall runs along the water's edge, and partway up the hill behind it stands the remains of an old house. The wooden roof has long since collapsed and now the walls of yellow stone are sur-rounded by weeds and bushes, inside and out. I wonder why the owner abandoned such a picturesque spot.

Beside me, Alberto snuffles in his sleep. He is lying on a blanket in the shade of a tree. Leaning down towards him, I look at his peaceful face. Not for the first time, I wonder what he will look like as an adult. Although he has his mother's eyes, his hair is fairer and curlier than hers, and his chin is stronger.

I always worried about the fact that the child would not look like me. Angelita soothed my fears, saying that the baby would have dark hair and dark eyes like all Spanish children. I'd laughed at her silliness, and hoped she was in part right.

Lying beside the sleeping child, I watch his small chest rise and fall rhythmically. I wonder what kind of man he will be. His mother was clever and funny and capable of enormous emotion. I am calm and steady, a man who likes routine and order. I have no idea what Alberto's real father was like. It will be interesting to see if he develops any characteristics that are neither his mother's nor mine. A blank slate or his personality already etched into his being: the classic debate will be played out in this little child — but I will be unable to discuss it with anyone.

Dispelling my scientific deliberation, I place a small kiss on the child's forehead and lay my head beside his. I need to think about the baptism. The water gurgles and bubbles nearby, and I feel the sun warm my legs.

Opening my eyes, I realize I must have dozed off. The blanket lies empty in front of me. Alberto is no longer on it. Panic rises from my stomach as I sit up quickly and call his name. Since he started walking, he has used his new skill at every opportunity. He's probably very close, I try to persuade myself as I get to my feet.

'Alberto!' I shout, and hear the fear in my voice.

I dash behind the nearby bushes. The little boy loves to play hide-and-seek, so perhaps he's playing now. But he's not. Running back to the blanket, I stand and look around. It's only now that I look towards the river.

A clamp grips my heart as I see a flash of white bobbing up and down on the dark water. For a moment, I cannot move; I cannot breathe. Then I force myself into action and run into the water, knocking the fishing rod over in my haste. The river quickly becomes deep, and as I wade out, the water comes up to my stomach.

As I get closer, I see Alberto is lying face down with his arms floating by his head. I pull his small body to me. He feels heavy and hangs limp in my arms as I drag myself back to the river's edge. Climbing out onto the sandy bank, I shake him and shout his name. His hair sticks to his head, and his sodden clothes cling to him. I don't know what to do. I shake him again, harder this time and his head wobbles.

Stop, I say to myself, taking a shaky breath. Think. Remember your anatomy. Water has filled the lungs. To expel it, apply pressure.

Carefully I place the child down on the blanket, lying him on his stomach, his head turned to the side. I kneel and place my hand on his back and gently push. Nothing happens. I lift my hand and apply pressure again onto the middle of his back. Still nothing. I feel the moment of calm reason start to lift from me and the panic slip back. I know I'm running out of time. Placing both hands on his back, I give the child's body a short, hard push.

Water gushes from Alberto's mouth, and I see his nose wrinkle as he gasps loudly. I gasp too and grapple him into my arms, turning him to look into his face. He coughs violently as yet more water dribbles from his nose and mouth, and his wide eyes look confused and frightened.

'Alberto,' I say quietly. 'Are you all right?'

He answers with a huge howl. I hold him tight and feel his deep sobs. As I rock and shush my crying child, I realize that even in my kneeling position, my legs are shaking so much that I have to sit down. We sit for a long time, and I continue to rock him long after his crying has stopped. The sun is starting to drop and the first of the midges are buzzing around us. The child looks up at me with tired eyes and I share his exhaustion.

'Alberto,' I whisper to him, 'I'm so sorry. I promise I'll never put you in danger again.' I turn my face to the pale blue sky.

'Angelita,' I say out loud, 'I'm sorry, my love, but you can't have him. He is not yours to take. He's mine now. And I will love him better than any father could.'

I look down at Alberto's face. He gazes up at me curiously.

'Let's go home,' I say gently to him. 'I have to speak to Father Sebastián.'

Chapter Thirteen

The boy whipped the air with a wild fennel stalk. Beside him, Alberto walked steadily along the rocky path. The unlaid road sloped gently upwards, and the old man looked at the green and grey hillside above them. If he were a younger man, he would have happily lived some- where like this.

The taxi had taken them to a town, where they'd caught a bus to a nearby village. There, they had asked for directions. They'd walked along a quiet road for about a mile; then, when they'd seen the top of a house nestled in the lowlands of a hill, they'd turned up the dirt track towards it. After sitting on the bus, it was good to be stretching their legs.

Soon they reached the house. All that was visible of it was the roof, as a tall white wall surrounded the build- ing. The wall itself could barely be seen under a spread of mature clematis and a thick undergrowth of bright yellow broom and wild onion. The branches of a kum- quat tree swung lazily over the wall, its trunk hidden on the other side. Heavy fruit hung from the branches. Alberto lifted the boy up so he could pick the shiny, olive-sized fruit. The boy took two, and when Alberto lowered him to the ground, he handed one to his grandfather.

Nodding to him, Alberto popped the whole fruit into his mouth, biting through the sweet skin to the tart pulp. Tino gnawed at the outside until only the bitter centre was left, which he threw into the bushes.

Alberto rang the bell beside a wooden door almost completely hidden behind a cluster of clematis flowers. Far away, a bell tinkled and instantly a dog started barking. Moving a woody vine, he saw an old sign, with the words PAN Y VINO burnt into the strip of hard-wood.

'"Bread and Wine,"' read Tino.

Alberto looked down at him and shrugged. The boy shrugged back, smiling.

At that moment, the door swung open. Alberto turned and saw a plump woman with white, curly hair smiling at him. She was wearing trousers and a straw hat, and held a pair of gardening gloves in one hand. A wiry, honey-coloured dog squirmed past her legs and, wagging its tail, tentatively sniffed at Alberto.

'Hello?' said the woman, looking first at Alberto and then at the boy.

'Hello!' said Tino, eyeing the dog with delight.

The old man nodded, suddenly bashful. He took his hat off and held it in front of his chest. 'Forgive the intrusion at your home,' he began quietly.

The woman smiled at him and brushed a curl from her face. The dog moved closer to the little boy, sniffing at his feet. Tino grinned and patted the dog's slim head.

'Are you Miriam Quintero?' Alberto asked quietly. He looked at her intently.

'Goodness,' she replied, chuckling, 'it's been a long time since anyone called me that. Yes, that was my name before I was married.'

Alberto nodded, uncomfortable. He looked down at the boy, who seemed to be holding his breath with excitement.

Turning back to Miriam, he said, 'I think we may have known each other when we were very young.'

'Yes?' replied Miriam curiously.

Alberto nodded again, turning his hat in his hands.

'My name is Alberto. Alberto Romero.'

Miriam stared at Alberto for a moment, the words sinking in. Then dropping the gloves, she slowly raised her hands to her mouth. Her eyes shone with confusion, and she blinked a number of times. She peered at the old man. Her eyes began to well with tears.

'Alberto?' she whispered through her fingers.

Alberto nodded. He could see she had recognized him despite the years. But when he looked at her face, he couldn't see the girl in the photo. He didn't know this woman.

Tentatively, Miriam stepped towards Alberto. She placed a hand on either side of his leathery face and gently kissed him on both cheeks. The tears were pouring down her face as she stepped back. The dog wound his way round her legs, eager for attention.

'We thought you were dead,' she said, her voice quivering.

Alberto looked at her, wishing he could remember.

Miriam wiped her eyes. 'And who is this?' she asked, looking at the boy.

'This is my grandson, Tino.'

Miriam smiled at the boy, then turned back to Alberto, looking into his face again.

'Well, you must both come in.'

'Thank you,' said Alberto.

With a click of her tongue, she nudged the dog towards the door and he bounded through.

The boy bent down, picked up Miriam's gloves and handed them to her. She smiled her thanks, then stepped to one side and, once the old man and the boy had crossed into the garden, shut the door behind them.

Alberto looked around. The garden was stunning. Along the house and exterior wall climbed jasmine and passion flower. The trunk of the kumquat tree was sturdy and leant heavily against the wall. Hibiscus, bandera with its Spanish-flag flowers, angel's trumpet and lilies covered the ground with small stone pathways running through them. Over the entrance to the house hung a spectacular mix of pink and red bougainvillea, and pots of fuchsia lined the steps leading up to the door. The mixture of scents was heady, and Alberto breathed them in deeply.

Miriam led them into the cool house, putting her gloves on a small table by the door. The dog's claws clicked on the tiled floor as he followed her.

'Please,' she said, indicating a large sofa, 'take a seat while I get us some drinks.'

Alberto and the boy sank into the soft cushions. Looking around, they saw a mix of old and new furniture set around the spacious room. Family photographs hung over the fireplace, and a pair of knitting needles stuck out of a bag by a comfy chair.

'Apu?'

'Yes.'

'Do you remember Señora Miriam?'

Alberto turned to the boy, who looked expectantly up at him. Sadly, he shook his head.

'Oh,' said Tino quietly.

Alberto rubbed the line of his jaw, his hard fingers rasping against the bristles. 'I wish I did,' he said.

When Miriam came through from the kitchen carrying a tray, Alberto stood and helped her put it on the table. She set a glass of sweet fizzy water in front of each of them and placed a bowl of olives in the centre of the table. Then she settled herself in the comfy chair opposite them and picked up her drink.

'Thank you,' said Alberto, lifting his glass.

The dog trotted up to the boy and flopped down

beside him. Grinning, the child stroked its ears and the dog's eyes closed with pleasure.

'I think he likes you,' said Miriam.

'What's his name?' asked the boy.

'Vito. Because he's always been so full of life.'

They all looked down at the dog, who leant against the boy's leg.

'I still can't believe it's you,' said Miriam, turning to Alberto. 'But it seems you don't remember me.'

Alberto slowly shook his head. 'I feel that I should, but I can't. I have lost my memory from those days.'

Miriam frowned. 'What do you remember?'

'I was taken to an orphanage, where I spent most of the war. There's very little before that. This one' – Alberto nodded and gestured towards his grandson – 'persuaded me to go looking for my history.'

Miriam smiled kindly at Tino.

'We went to where the orphanage was, but there was a mean old man there,' said the boy. 'Then we met Doña Isabel, and we went to the church. Then Apu saw a bottle of brandy and we went to the vineyard and saw the cellar. Then they said to come here.'

'Well,' said Miriam, 'it sounds like you've had quite an adventure!'

The little boy grinned and nodded before gulping down more of his drink.

'The new owners of Quintero's gave us your address,' explained Alberto.

'Ah,' said Miriam.

'Apu,' said the boy excitedly, 'don't forget the photos!'

Alberto opened his bag, which lay by his feet. He took out the photos and handed them to Miriam.

'Oh!' she said. 'Look at these – so long ago.' She leafed through them until she got to the one Javier had shown them. Smiling, she turned it to show Alberto.

'This is when we were very young. This is my brother, Néstor,' she said, pointing to the teenage boy. 'And of course this is me, and our mother and father. Do you remember any of us?'

'No. There's something there, a glimmer, but it's not clear.' He looked at the photo again. 'Your father looks like a good man.'

Miriam smiled and nodded. 'He was. A very good man. That vineyard was everything to him. He'd be so sad to know that it had been sold. But he left it to Néstor and my brother was never interested. He'd rather have a beer than a glass of wine.

'My father's name was Dante,' Miriam continued. 'He passed away not long after this photo was taken. He and your father were very good friends.'

'My father?' said Alberto quietly.

'Yes. You don't remember him either?'

Alberto shook his head.

'Oh, Alberto, that's sad. I remember him a little. He was very kind and clever – a real gentleman.'

'A gentleman?'

'Yes. He was quietly spoken and polite. And he smiled a great deal. He always had time for us children. I'm sorry, it's not much – but I was very young.'

Alberto shrugged. It didn't matter. It seemed there were no memories to trigger.

'Did he work for your father?'

'Yes, that's right.'

'In the fields?'

'Oh no! He was a chemist. He helped develop the wines. My father was quite advanced in employing a scientist, and your father introduced some new ways of testing and processing the wine. It was the two of them that started the brandy production.'

'And did we live at Quintero's?' asked Alberto.

'Yes, that's right,' said Miriam enthusiastically. 'You and your father lived in a casita out the back of the main building. You used to come into the house and have meals with us.'

'And my mother?' asked Alberto.

'Oh, Alberto,' said Miriam gently. 'I'm afraid I never knew her. Neither did you – she died at your birth.'

Alberto looked down at his clasped hands and sat very still.

Tino regarded his grandfather sadly.

The old man took a deep breath. It seemed there were nuggets of information, important things that he should recall. His father's character, his mother's death – these things should be scorched on his memory. Yet here he was, his family and his past within his grasp, and he still couldn't remember the woman sitting in front of him.

'I'm sorry,' said Alberto. 'It's difficult learning it all as if for the first time.'

'I'm sure,' said Miriam sympathetically. She picked up the bowl of olives and held them out to the small boy. He chose the largest one he could see and quickly popped it into his mouth.

Miriam set the bowl back on the table, putting an olive into her own mouth as she leant back in her chair. As he looked up, Alberto saw the olive dribble a fat dollop of oil onto Miriam's ample chest. Miriam followed Alberto's gaze and glanced down. A large stain marked her white top. Her face fell.

'Oh,' she said in exasperation, 'can you believe it? This was clean this morning. I'm always doing this.'

Alberto's eyes darted between the stain and Miriam's perturbed face. As she pulled out a handkerchief and dabbed at the oil, he watched her face. Then he looked at the stain again.

'Mimi?' he said quietly.

Miriam stopped dabbing and turned to him.

'Mimi,' said Alberto with more conviction.

Miriam nodded slowly at him.

Alberto stood up and stepped round the table towards her. Miriam stood to face him.

'Mimi,' said Alberto hoarsely, 'my friend.'

Smiling through her tears, Mimi nodded again at

Alberto. The old man stood uncomfortably in front of her, before Mimi pulled him to her and they hugged.

The little boy grinned and gave Vito a hug.

Mimi watched the boy climbing up the stone terrace to where Vito waited for him. She tutted and shook her head. 'Poor child,' she said.

Alberto had just told her about Juan Carlos's accident and the boy's reaction to his father's situation. The child had slept well and without nightmares both nights they had been away.

'You must phone your daughter as soon as we get home,' said Mimi firmly.

Together, Alberto and Mimi strolled along the terraces that led from the back of her house. Gnarled olive trees were spaced evenly along the wide terrace, and their feet sank gently into the soft crust of brown earth.

Tino and the dog scampered up and down the ancient walls. Above them, the hill rose, the terraces petering out to bushes and craggy boulders. The sun was starting to lose its strength, and a gentle breeze swept over them.

Mimi had suggested a walk before dinner. At her insistence, Alberto had agreed they would stay the night. She had a big house, and now that her husband was no longer alive and the children had left, she had more than enough space for them both.

As they walked, they talked of their lives since the war. Alberto avoided talk of their childhood. It felt as if the recognition of Mimi, the little girl who was his best friend as a child, had opened the door a crack. He worried that with a push, the door would fly open and the torrent of memories that flooded out would sink him. For now, he wanted to keep the surge at bay.

Instead, he learnt that Mimi had been lucky enough to go to college and study business. She had hoped Néstor would let her help run Quintero's after their father died. She had ideas to grow and modernize the business. But her brother had refused, saying there was no need for change — they would carry on as always. He agreed with Franco that a woman's place was in the home, not at work. Mimi had argued that their father had always been progressive, but Néstor had left all the business affairs to his foreman. Mimi had known the foreman and considered him lazy with little passion for the business.

It was with great difficulty, Mimi told Alberto, that she had walked away from Quintero's. She took a job in a leather shoe company that made workmen's boots. It was hard and she'd had to fight for her independence at a time when the government had been against women in the workplace. But she gained the respect of the bosses and they had given her greater responsibility. After years of persuasion, she eventually convinced them to develop fashion shoes. She found a young designer, and thanks to her shrewd business instinct and Franco's plan to make Spain a modern economy, the shoe company had grown to become the best known in the area.

It was during this time she met her husband. He was an accountant: safe and reliable but with a sharp wit and a big laugh. After the marriage, she continued to work at the shoe company but just one or two days a week. However, when she had her third child, she decided that running the family kept her busy enough.

She had brought up three boys, all of whom had gone to university, and one, she proudly admitted, had become a politician. Her husband had died young, in his fifties. She had never considered remarrying; instead, she put her energy into her garden and her family.

'I am content, Alberto,' she said. 'I have had a wonderful life — and I'm enjoying my older years. And now your arrival — well, I couldn't have asked for a more wonderful surprise.'

'And I am glad to have found you,' replied Alberto.

As Mimi fried green peppers in the kitchen, Alberto and his grandson called Rosa. She said that Juan Carlos's recovery had been remarkable.

The doctors had warned both Juan Carlos and Rosa that the healing process would be long and painful, but the prognosis was excellent.

Alberto could hear the relief in his daughter's voice. She said her sister, Cristina, would be leaving the next day, and her mother-in-law was spending less time at the hospital. She joked that Juan Carlos had pleaded for his mother to watch her beloved soap operas at home rather than in his hospital room.

The boy was excited to hear about his father's progress and asked several questions. Then he filled her in on everything he and his grandfather had learnt and talked to his mother at length about Vito and asked if they could get a dog. His mother replied that when things calmed down, they would talk about it. The boy raced off to tell Mimi, Vito bouncing after him, barking.

'Do you know what you have done?' asked the old man, smiling down the phone.

'Oh, Papá, all this has made me realize there's more to life than worrying about dog hairs. Of course, we'll have to wait until Juan Carlos is well enough.'

'Boys and dogs are a good match,' said Alberto.

'And how about you? It sounds as if you are having quite an adventure! How does it feel to uncover your history?'

'It's unsettling,' he admitted.

He was going to go on, but Rosa interrupted, 'Papá?'

'Yes?'

'When will you be coming home?'

Alberto could hear Rosa's ache for her son in her voice. Alberto sighed silently. Mimi had invited them to stay for a few days. She and Alberto could catch up properly, and the boy and Vito would enjoy each other's company. He had said it would depend on his daughter. Now, listening to her voice, he knew they had to go back.

'Tomorrow, Rosa. We'll come home tomorrow.'

'Oh, Papá, don't come if you're still searching. I wouldn't want you to cut your trip short.'

'No, no. I've found everything here at Mimi's,' said Alberto softly.

Mimi placed the steaming tortilla on the kitchen table. It was thick and golden with flecks of green pepper running through it. Tino took a deep breath, taking in the rich smell of the eggy potato pie.

She handed Alberto a bottle of wine, which he opened, the cork releasing from the neck with a satisfying sound.

While he poured the wine, Mimi served the boy, who sat, distracted by Vito.

'Vito,' said Mimi in a reproving tone.

The dog turned his large dark eyes to his mistress, but after one look at her determined face, got up and trotted, defeated, to his bed in the corner of the room.

'Eat your dinner,' said the old man to the boy.

'One moment, Alberto,' said Mimi firmly. She finished serving herself and sat down. Closing her eyes and clasping her hands together, she dropped her head. The boy squeezed his eyes tight shut, and Alberto lowered his head.

As Mimi said a short grace, even Vito stopped noisily licking himself and lay still. When she had finished, she nodded at the boy, who hungrily tucked into his meal.

Alberto and Mimi sipped the wine. 'It's a Quintero,' said Mimi.

'I saw,' said Alberto.

'It's from one of our best years, not long before my

father died. I have a collection of wines that the vineyard gave me.'

'Yes, the new owner told me. That was how we found you.'

'My father always talked so passionately about the wine. He loved every part of the process, and I believe his heart is in every glass.'

Alberto took another sip and nodded. It was very good.

'So your son-in-law is improving?' asked Mimi.

'Yes. He's doing very well.'

'Do you think you may stay a few more days?'

Alberto paused a moment, before sadly shaking his head. 'Thank you for your kind offer, but my daughter is missing Tino. He's her only child . . .'

Mimi raised her hand. 'There's no need to explain, Alberto. The wonderful thing is that now you've found me, you can visit again. Or I could come to visit you.'

'Will you bring Vito?' asked the boy quickly. The dog lifted his head at the sound of his name.

'Of course,' said Mimi. 'I think Vito would like to see the sea.'

The boy nodded happily as he took another mouthful of tortilla.

'So, Alberto, have you been a gardener all your life?' Mimi asked.

Alberto nodded. 'My education wasn't good, so I took work where I could find it after the war — labouring on building sites, working on farms at harvest time. I was always happier outside. When I met María Luisa on her family's olive farm, I learnt a great deal about agriculture. For our wedding, her father bought us a small plot of land. I grew crops to sell, and for our table.

'Then the tourists began to arrive in the area. They bought and built villas with gardens and plenty of land, but they only stayed in them for a few months a year. María Luisa knew a woman who sold properties to the British and Dutch. Through her, my wife began work as a cleaner – looking after the empty houses and preparing them for their owners' return.

'And I was hired to look after the gardens and the land. Often, the villas came with many terraces of almonds and olive trees. They paid me to maintain them, and often allowed me to take the harvest.

'Some of the families returned over many years, and María Luisa became friends with a few of them. She would show the wives the best places to shop and would learn a few words of their language. If they were interested, I would show the men how to clear the irrigation channels and check for termites in their villas' woodwork.

'María Luisa became good friends with one English family. They spoke a little Spanish and liked to learn the Spanish way of life. One day every summer, María Luisa would make a large paella, and we would carry it up to their house on a hill. Our two families would eat together and the children played, despite none of them speaking the same language. I made their youngest child

— a little *rubia* — her own garden. It had a lemon tree and flowers that would be in bloom when the family arrived.'

Alberto smiled at the memories.

'It's interesting you've always worked with plants, Alberto. Have you ever worked with grapes?' asked Mimi.

'Only picking them at harvest time. I did make my own wine once, but even I could barely drink it,' he chuckled.

'I wonder what would have happened if you had stayed at Quintero's. Papá always wanted you to help Néstor run the vineyard — just as your father helped him. But while your father was a scientist, it sounds as if you could have appreciated my father's love of the vine. You would have been a better foreman than the lazy waster my brother hired.'

Alberto shrugged. 'What if the war had not come? What if Néstor had given you Quintero's? What if? We have lived the lives we have lived.'

Mimi nodded. 'Of course you're right. But part of me wonders if, when you lost your memory, some of my father's words remained. He was always talking to us about plants — perhaps somehow a little of his know-ledge settled in your memory. It's a nice thought to have. It would have made him happy.'

They all sat in silence for a moment.

'Aunt Mimi?' said the boy earnestly.

'Yes, dear,' Mimi smiled at him.

'Do you know when Apu's birthday is?'

Mimi looked at Alberto. 'You don't remember your birthday?'

He shook his head.

'Oh dear. Let me think. My father liked any excuse for a fiesta, so we would have celebrated your birthday. We were similar in age, you and I, but while my birthday is in June, I'm afraid I can't remember yours.'

The little boy's face fell.

'I'm sorry — both of you.'

Alberto gave Mimi a small smile. 'Don't worry, Mimi. The reason we came on this journey was to find my birthday. But' — he turned to his grandson — 'because of this journey I have found my oldest friend. And I have found some of my memories. I remember playing in the cellars at Quintero's. I remember the warm kitchen that always smelt of food. They're not crystal clear; they're a bit blurry — but they're my memories.' Reaching out, Alberto stroked the boy's head. 'And I have you to thank for that.'

Tino looked at his grandfather and smiled.

'Wait,' said Mimi suddenly.

As they both turned, she stood up and left the room. Vito lifted his head and watched her go, then laid his head back down, his eyebrows twitching.

The boy turned to Alberto with a questioning look and the old man shrugged.

When Mimi returned, she held an old leather-bound book in her hand. She stood in front of Alberto and held it out to him.

Before he could take it, a thin piece of card fell from the book and fluttered onto the floor, landing in front of Vito, who quickly sniffed it with his wet nose.

The boy leant down from his chair and picked up the card. Turning it in his fingers, he revealed a photo of a woman. She was young and attractive with warm, dark eyes, and although the picture was serious, a smile danced around her lips.

'Who's that, Apu?'

Alberto carefully took the old photo, shaking his head. 'I don't know,' he said.

'Alberto,' said Mimi quietly. 'That's your mother.'

The old man caught his breath. He stared at the photo, bringing it closer to his eyes. Immediately, he could see similarities — the shape of her face, her nose, but, most strikingly, her eyes were just like his.

Alberto let out a short breath. The more he looked at the photo, the more familiar it seemed. As if he had seen it many times before.

Turning the photo over, Alberto looked for writing on the smudged paper. There was nothing.

Reading his mind, Mimi said, 'Her name was Angelita.'

'Angelita,' repeated the old man softly.

'Little Angel,' said the boy.

'I kept this to remind me of you,' said Mimi, giving Alberto the book in her hands. 'At first, I kept everything I could — your toys, your schoolbooks, all sorts of things. But over the years, I let them go. When I left home, this was the only thing of yours that I kept. And I have kept it all these years.'

Carefully, the old man turned the book in his hands. Its dark red cover was faded, and the gold edging of the paper only shone in patches. A tatty red ribbon hung from the middle pages. The words HOLY BIBLE were embossed simply on the front cover.

Very slowly, Alberto opened it, releasing a musty smell. An inscription was written in tidy letters on the first page.

> *To Alberto,*
> *With blessings for a happy and healthy life.*
> *From your father*

Chapter Fourteen

FATHER FRANCISCO
21 July 1931

The mule's ears twitch as it pulls the cart. The peasant beside me seems to have dozed off, but the animal plods on regardless. I'm glad for the peace to gather my thoughts.

It's been three months since the king's abdication and the repercussions are now becoming obvious. A Republic will soon be announced, and the country will be governed by a doctrine that separates State and Church. I, like many of my brethren, am concerned.

But for now, I can put my worries to one side, as I am on my way to visit my old friend Father Sebastián. We worked together in the city many years ago, and have been in touch from time to time, but this will be the first time we've seen each other in many years.

I assume he has heard of my new posting, and the recent tragic events, through the bishop. I'm unsure I can talk about it yet, but I am looking forward to seeing him again.

Without instruction, the mule veers off the road and onto a small path. The man beside me snores gently. I consider waking him, but the animal seems to know where it's going.

It is late morning and the sun is at full strength. My black robes and hat are devilishly hot and not for the first time I wonder who decided on black for our uniform. After all, I don't believe our Lord Jesus wore black — he lived in a hot country too.

All around us, the land is dry and dusty. The summer has been harsh so far, and, as in my village, the people here will be wishing for some unseasonable but welcome rain. There is not a breath of wind. Apart from the regular clomp of the mule's hoofs and the occasional bird, it is deathly quiet.

In the distance, I see a small cluster of houses and buildings. That must be Father Sebastián's town. I realize I am looking forward to being somewhere other than my own home. I have lived in the village for only a few months, but it has been an extremely difficult time. I am pleased to be away from there for a few days.

As we approach the town, I see a few women walking towards us. I nudge the driver awake and instruct him to stop, and they come close enough for me to touch their scarfed heads. I ask them where they are going and they reply shyly that they are going home after market. They point to their meagre bundles wrapped on their backs — the week's simple purchases. They smile at me, revealing missing teeth, and continue on their way. It seems impossible to think that the Church is so threatened by the poor.

We head into the centre of the town and past the small market, now packing up. The driver directs the docile mule up a small street behind the back of the church. We stop outside a large house and my companion points to the door. Thanking him, I let him hand me my bag as I climb down.

I pull the chain and deep inside the house I hear a bell ring. The mule clip-clops up the cobbled street. The driver looks ready for another siesta, and I imagine that he will be happy to go wherever the mule decides to take him.

The door opens and an elderly woman stands in the doorway. 'Father Francisco,' she says politely. 'Welcome.'

She opens the door and lets me into the dark reception room. 'Father Sebastián is expecting you,' she says, leading me down the corridor. The house may be large, but it is simply furnished. Father Sebastián, like me, abhors the ostentatious homes some priests have. For Sebastián, I believe it is a question of style – his being modest and unassuming. For me, I would prefer church funds were used to help the poor than dress a house unnecessarily.

The woman knocks on the door at the end of the corridor and waits for a response. I recognize Sebastián's deep voice instantly and I feel myself relax. The woman opens the door and there, walking towards me, is my old friend.

Portly and red-cheeked, he has put on some weight, but it is so good to see him I decide not to remark on it. He seems pleased to see me as we shake hands.

'Welcome, Francisco,' he says warmly. Then, 'Señora,' he says over my shoulder, 'please bring lunch at your convenience.'

The woman nods and closes the door behind her. It is only one o'clock, so I am surprised to hear of eating already, but the journey has been long and I realize I am hungry.

'How was the trip?' asks Sebastián. He points me towards a comfortable chair.

'Good, thank you,' I reply. 'But extremely hot.'

There's a knock on the door and the señora enters with a small tray. She places a glass of water beside me and gives us each a crystal glass of light sherry before putting the bottle on the table beside Sebastián. He thanks her and she quietly leaves the room.

'So good to see you, friend,' says Sebastián. He smiles and raises his glass. We drink the cool, sharp sherry and pass pleasantries, until there's a second knock on the door and the señora enters again. She carries another tray to the large oak table and starts laying out food. When she has finished, Sebastián and I rise from our chairs and cross to the table. After a brief blessing, Sebastián pours wine from a decanter, while I look at the spread before us.

'What a generous table of food, Sebastián,' I say.

'I am grateful for all I receive,' he replies, smiling.

'And what will you do if the rumours are true and the government stops paying our salaries?' I ask.

'Oh, dear friend, I had to buy very little of this food. Most of it is gifted to me by my loyal congregation.'

I nod, watching him take a large mouthful of asparagus and roasted red pepper. He certainly has won the support of the area's richest families.

Teasing him a little, I say, 'Perhaps the Church should stand alongside the poor — make a difference where we can.'

'Perhaps, Francisco,' says Sebastián, easing back in his seat and smiling at me. 'And perhaps you should have followed your namesake and become a Franciscan monk.'

'I'm not about to give up my boots, Sebastián,' I reply. 'But you know this new Republic poses a very great threat to us — whatever your political point of view. It plans to stop all religious education and ban all religious processions — even the ringing of church bells.'

He looks at me, appalled. 'No church bells in Spain, Francisco?'

'They want change. And change is not convincing unless everyone can see and hear it. They call the new Republic "the Beautiful Child". They've given birth to something they believe is a force for good. I think the only way to survive is to join them in raising their beautiful child.'

He refills his glass and swirls the wine thoughtfully. 'How did it come to this, Francisco?'

'We've been too comfortable for too long, friend,' I reply gently. 'We've become complacent and forgotten our vows. These days, the Spanish Church would most likely consider Christ a Marxist.'

'Hush,' says Sebastián with a laugh. 'You will land yourself in trouble if you're not careful.'

I smile at him. He is a good man. Mild-mannered and easy-going, he joined the Church for an easy life – as a great many men do. I do not think he is prepared for what may be coming.

'Here, comrade,' says Sebastián. He refills my glass. 'Have another glass of wine with me before you join the revolution.'

It is still humid and warm despite the late hour. A fat, red ball of sun is just about to set behind the far, hazy mountains. I hear Sebastián huffing behind me and slow my pace.

'I don't know why you wouldn't let us take the cart,' says Sebastián. He pats his forehead with a handkerchief.

'I think we both needed some fresh air, friend,' I reply. After an afternoon of eating, drinking and conversing, we had both dozed off in our chairs. Unlike Sebastián, I am unaccustomed to drinking so heartily and awoke feeling thick-headed and slow; when he asked me to help him talk to one of his parishioners, I agreed, pleased to stretch my legs.

Up ahead is a large hacienda. It's an attractive building, and the lines of vines alongside us are well kept.

'What did you say the owner's name was?' I ask.

This gives Sebastián a moment to pause and get his breath. 'Don Dante,' he replies. 'His family have had this vineyard for over one hundred and fifty years. He's very popular in the area. He looks after his workers and is well respected by both them and his customers. I'm sure you'll approve of him.'

I smile at Sebastián. He must think I am far too opinionated for a cleric.

'But it is Raúl I have come to see,' says Sebastián.

'His son?'

'No, his chemist.'

I turn to Sebastián with a quizzical look.

'It's a sad story. Raúl and his wife arrived about a year ago. Dante was looking for someone to help him improve his wine and was open to a little experimenta-tion. Raúl was looking for a job away from the city and they became friends instantly. Dante swears he saw the value of the scientist's contribution very quickly.

'I believe the wife was pregnant when they arrived — a beautiful young woman. I rarely saw her, though. She never came to Mass in all those months. Raúl made excuses for her, but I spoke to Dante about it once. He said she had fallen out of love with religion. It was his opinion that with a little time, she would grow to love it again. She never got the chance. She died in childbirth a few months ago.'

I tut sadly, and for a while we walk in silence.

'And the baby?' I ask eventually.

'Healthy and well,' says Sebastián.

'Excellent.'

'But I am concerned that the father hasn't spoken to me about the baptism yet,' he says.

'Do you think it has something to do with the mother's opinion of religion?' I ask.

'It shouldn't matter,' he says flatly. 'It's his decision now.'

'Perhaps he just needs a little time,' I say.

'After all you've said about the decline of Catholicism in the masses,' says Sebastián seriously, 'surely you think we should make every effort to bring all the children we can into the arms of the Church? That baby should be baptized — the sooner the better.'

'*And now why tarriest thou? Arise, and be baptized, and wash away thy sins, calling on the name of the Lord*,' I quote, quietly.

'Exactly! Don't you remember when we all worked at the children's hospital in the city? Antonio would baptize newborns in case they didn't survive. Most of their parents would have objected given the chance, but he thought saving their souls was more important.'

At the mention of Antonio's name, I fall silent. This visit has, in part, helped me escape what has been a difficult time.

Sebastián notices and puts a hand on my shoulder. 'What happened?' he asks. I realize he has probably been wanting to ask about our mutual friend since my arrival.

I take a deep breath. 'I truly don't know why he did

it. I don't believe I'll ever understand, despite knowing him so well.'

Antonio and I had become friends at the seminary when we began our training. I had chosen the Church; Antonio's family expected it of him. It was me he turned to when, as happened from time to time, he questioned his faith. He worried that he would not live up to what was expected of him. We talked about ideology a great deal, but he rarely seemed to find the answers he was looking for.

After college, we had been sent to work in a hospital in the city, where we met Sebastián. We were shocked to find just how extreme the poverty was — and the poorer the area, the smaller the church attendance. It was hard work, but at last, Antonio had found some contentment in his situation.

He had moved some years later. A priest had passed away and Antonio was asked to take over a church situated in quite a wealthy part of town. We met occasionally after that, but I had to admit I noticed a change in him. He became distant and uncommunicative, and I sensed his demons had returned. At times, he was angry, furious with himself and with God. At other times, he was overwhelmed by remorse, pleading for forgiveness from his sins.

The last time I'd seen him, he'd told me he was leaving the parish. He said he had requested a new post. He said his current position had made him question his faith again — in fact, it had pushed what faith he had to

its limit. He thought if he could go somewhere different, somewhere that he was really needed again, it would
help him find a way back to God.

He'd been granted a position in the rural village
where I now live. I promised to visit as soon as I could,
but I never had the chance.

A few months ago, I had been summoned in the
middle of the night. The bishop had sent his car and
I was driven to the village. The bishop himself met me
there. He told me that the church custodian had found
Antonio that evening. He had hanged himself.

I sigh at the memory and say, 'You know almost as
much as I do, Sebastián.'

'I only know that he took his own life, and that you
have now taken over his parish.'

'When the bishop arrived, he discovered that Antonio had left a letter. It was addressed to me, so the bishop
had me brought to the village.

'But when I read the suicide note, it revealed little.
It thanked me for being such a good friend and begged
my forgiveness. He gave no explanation as to why he had
been driven to this terrible deed. It had simply said that
he was not worthy of being a priest.'

'Where was he laid to rest?' asks Sebastián.

'In the churchyard.'

Sebastián gasps. 'But, Francisco, it's a mortal sin.'

'The bishop wanted his body to be returned to his
family. But they are wealthy with strong connections to
the Church. It would have ruined them to bury their

shamed son. The bishop wanted the problem to go away and I suggested that we bury him in the churchyard in an unmarked grave.'

'Well, I still don't know,' says Sebastián.

'He was our friend,' I say gently.

Sebastián wipes his head with his handkerchief and nods, then gestures for me to continue.

'I then asked the bishop if I could stay on. I felt I owed it to Antonio. I wanted to be where he had suffered so much. And if his spirit remained in some state of purgatory, I could maybe help him.'

'The devil must have been whispering in his ear to commit such a sin,' says Sebastián.

'I don't know,' I reply. 'I don't think we'll ever know. Perhaps it pays to remember that we are only men. Weak and sinful men.'

'If Antonio's spirit remains in the church, I can't feel it,' I continue. 'But every day I pray for him.'

'May God bless him,' says Sebastián.

We approach the front of the house, and Sebastián leads me through an arch into a courtyard. There, a man with a round, kindly face is bouncing a baby on his knee. He beams when he sees us and stands, shifting the baby onto his side. 'Welcome, welcome,' he says cheerily.

Sebastián introduces me and the man – Dante – shakes my hand warmly. 'You are welcome. This is little Mimi,' he says, proudly holding up the child. Sebastián chucks her under the chin.

'Come inside and have a drink,' says Dante.

We step into the warm house, and Dante leads me through to the kitchen. There, sitting at a large table, is a middle-aged woman, her hair wrapped in a scarf. She is holding another baby.

Dipping her head to us, she stands and carries the baby to a Moses basket, where she settles him.

'Father Francisco, have you had far to come?' Dante asks.

I explain where my village is, and we discuss the journey for a while. Sipping the wine, I compliment Dante on its flavour.

'Thank you,' he says. 'I put it down to a satisfying blend of generations of experience and a modern approach to winemaking.'

The door clicks open and I turn to see a young man enter the room. His face looks aged beyond its years, and dark circles lie under his eyes. He is unshaven, and his shirt is crumpled. I can only assume this is Raúl.

'Aha,' cries Dante, 'Raúl, you know Father Sebastián, and this is Father Francisco, who is currently visiting.'

Raúl hides his initial look of surprise with a tired smile.

'How are you, Raúl?' asks Sebastián.

'Fine, thank you, Father,' he replies. It is clear he is not.

'Chita?' he says to the woman as he walks towards the baby in the basket.

'Alberto's fine. I'm just preparing his milk now.'

The young man picks the baby up and, holding him gently, stares into his eyes. Then he pulls the child tightly to him, his own eyes closed firmly.

'Raúl?' says Sebastián gently.

After a moment, the man opens his eyes and looks at the priest.

'When would you like me to perform his baptism?'

A dark look passes over Raúl's face, but he is silent.

'I said, when would you like—' repeats my friend.

'I heard you, Father,' says the man.

'Well?'

After some thought, Raúl says, 'When I am ready to organize Alberto's christening, I would be honoured if you would perform the ceremony.'

There is a silence; we are all aware that Raúl is procrastinating.

'Raúl, I know you've been through a great trauma . . .' urges Sebastián.

The young man shakes his head, as if to dispel an annoying voice inside it.

'But,' continues Sebastián, 'this child is ready to be released from original sin.'

'No,' says Raúl weakly.

'It is for Alberto's salvation,' says Sebastián with force.

'No!' shouts Raúl.

The room is still, stunned at this outburst. Raúl buries his head into his son's neck, clearly overcome with grief. As we watch, he takes a deep breath, smelling the baby's sweet scent. For this moment, his world is his son.

Awkwardly, Sebastián reaches out to stroke the child's hair but stops himself. Instead, his gaze directed firmly at the heartbroken young man in front of him, he says softly, 'Forgive me, Raúl.'

Raúl looks up bleary-eyed at the priest and slowly nods.

All of us stand uncomfortably until Dante says, 'Father Sebastián, would you care to see our new casks?'

Sebastián gratefully accepts the invitation, and handing his daughter to Chita, Dante gently leads him out of the kitchen.

'You've done the right thing,' says Chita to Raúl.

I pour him a glass of wine from the bottle on the table and pass it to him. He takes it with a suspicious glance towards me.

'There is no rush,' I say. He is clearly surprised by my words and he nods gratefully at me, but just as he is about to respond, Mimi hiccups and vomits milk over herself and Chita.

'I'll have to change her again.' The woman sighs, walking towards the door.

As she leaves, Raúl smiles. 'She's always doing that.'

I smile back at him, glad that the mood has relaxed.

'Are you all right?' I ask.

'Fine,' he replies.

'I imagine you've said you're fine a great deal over the past few months, when you really aren't.'

Raúl looks me in the eye before returning his attention to baby Alberto.

'Sebastián has told me of your situation and I am sorry for your loss,' I say to him. After years of being a priest, these are words that come easily. But I feel for this man. He looks as if the life has been sucked out of him.

He shrugs and I can see he believes that my words are well meant but insincere.

'I recently lost a very close friend,' I say. 'I have never been married, but I understand the pain of loss.'

Raúl looks at me.

Reaching for my satchel, I pull out a book. It is a Bible. In fact, it is Antonio's Bible. I have been carrying it with me since I found it among his possessions. It is beautiful in its simplicity – a dark red cover and gold-edged pages.

'Raúl, this has been a comfort to me in dark times. Now I hope it helps you as it has me.' I hand the Bible to Raúl, who takes it cautiously.

'And I believe that one day you will be ready to have Alberto baptized. Please accept this gift for him on that day. If you decide not to have him baptized, please give the Bible to him when he's old enough to read it and understand it. That way, you place the decision in his own hands.'

Raúl turns the book, thoughtfully, before looking at me. 'Thank you,' he says.

'Would you like me to bless Alberto before we leave?' I ask.

Raúl smiles down at the baby. The child responds with a gurgle that makes Raúl grin. 'I think a blessing would be fine,' he says.

Chapter Fifteen

'Alberto,' said Mimi gently, 'do you remember anything about the day you went missing?'

The old man shook his head. He wasn't entirely sure he wanted to remember. That day had changed the course of his life. He could have been part of that comfortable family in the photo. Instead, he had been on his own, all through the years at the orphanage and then his young adult life. Until María Luisa.

Taking a deep breath, Alberto looked at Mimi. This was why he had come on this journey. This was the memory that had been missing for most of his life. Mimi was the only person who could tell him. It had been sixty-five years. It was time.

'Please,' Alberto said hoarsely, 'can you tell me?'

Mimi nodded at Alberto, then topped up his glass of wine. The boy had gone to bed, and Vito was curled up outside his bedroom door. The house was quiet and calm.

Mimi chewed her lip absent-mindedly, as if trying to decide where to begin. Alberto waited.

'Well,' she started carefully, 'you and your father

went for a drive. He had a big, old car that he adored. It was late afternoon, and you both left in the car. But you never came back.'

'Where were we going?'

'I don't know,' said Mimi. She stumbled a little over the words.

Alberto looked at Mimi. She shook her head and sighed.

'We were playing. You, me and Néstor. There was an argument and you and Néstor had a fight. Your father came and took you off for a drive – to ease the situation.'

'What was the argument about?'

'Oh, nothing. Childish things,' said Mimi. She looked into her glass.

Alberto looked at Mimi and recalled that his friend had always been a terrible liar. 'Mimi, I've come so far for this. Please tell me the truth.'

Mimi looked at him and gave a deep sigh. Reluctantly, she began to speak again. 'Néstor was not a nice child. He was jealous of our friendship – you and me. Being a little bit younger, he was always trying to keep up with us. My parents, too, must take some of the blame. My father always wanted a boy, and he and my mother spoilt Néstor.' Mimi took a sip of her wine, then continued, 'He was mean to me that day. And you defended me.'

As Alberto listened to Mimi talk, he saw images in his mind's eye to match the words. He saw the courtyard dappled in light. He saw Néstor push Mimi to the ground. He saw his own reaction.

'I hit him,' said Alberto softly.

'You remember?' asked Mimi quickly.

Alberto nodded. He saw Néstor sitting on the ground, blood dripping from his nose onto his white shirt. He saw Néstor say something, saw his mouth move, but he couldn't hear the words. He sensed a rage; then he was standing over Néstor, punching and kicking him with all his strength. Then large hands grasped him and pulled him away from the boy.

'What did he say' — Alberto looked at Mimi — 'to make me so angry?'

She paused, unsure whether to speak.

'Mimi, he said something to me. What was it?'

Mimi breathed in deeply. 'He said that your father was not your real father.'

Alberto saw the scene again, and this time he could hear Néstor's words as they came from his mouth.

You're a bastard.

The old man caught his breath. He winced and closed his eyes. As Mimi watched him, Alberto rubbed his chest distractedly.

'Are you all right?' said Mimi, concerned.

Alberto opened his eyes and looked at her. 'I'm fine,' he whispered. He leant back in his chair.

'After you left, we never spoke of it again. Néstor hid in his room for days. And although my parents asked repeatedly, neither of us said a word.'

Mimi continued, 'A soldier came the next day to say your father's car had been found. It had crashed and then caught fire. They gave my father your father's papers. They were half burnt, but they were definitely his. The soldier said your father had been thrown from the vehicle and had died in the blaze. When my father asked about you, the soldier said you must have perished too.

'My father wanted to go and look for himself — just in case. But the soldier said the area was very dangerous — the fighting was spreading. And he said no one inside the car could have possibly survived. My mother pleaded with Papá not to go, and in the end he agreed.

'I'm so sorry, Alberto. They truly thought you had died in the car. If I'd known, I would have begged my father to go and search for you. And he would have. He adored you.

'Instead, we learnt to live with the fact that you and your father were dead. Even Néstor was upset — he blamed himself. He was only a boy. Who could have known a moment of childish spitefulness would have such repercussions?'

Alberto frowned. Memories suddenly overwhelmed him — not just the argument, but the drive with his father and more.

Mimi reached across the table and put her hand on top of his.

Alberto looked up at her and said, 'You wouldn't have found me anyway.'

'What?' said Mimi.

'If you and your father had come to the car to look for me, I wouldn't have been there.'

Now he could see it. All of it. The memories were crystal clear, as if they'd been sealed in a vacuum and now released.

Alberto took a deep breath and started to speak.

'After the fight with Néstor, my father took me to his car. We drove in silence. We were heading in the direction of the river, where he used to take us fishing.

'But then we started talking. He asked why I hit your brother. For a long time I was silent, but he kept asking. I think he knew the answer, but he wanted me to say it. In the end, I did. I said that Néstor had called me a bastard.

'It was then that we missed the turning for the river. I don't think my father noticed until we were quite a long way past it. And then he just carried on, whichever way the road took us. He just drove. And we talked.

'He said that it was true. That he wasn't my real father. But that he was proud to be the man I called "Papá". He said he had treated me as his own son, and intended to as long as God gave him breath in his body.

'Of course, I asked him who my father was. He said he didn't know. My mother had had an affair, and it was a man she loved deeply, but he had left her. She had turned to my father then, and was only a few months pregnant when he married her. He told me my mother never spoke of the man again. She had never spoken to anyone of him.

'He said he was sorry. He was sorry about the way I had found out. He was sorry I had never been able to meet my mother or talk to her about it. He said he hoped it would not tarnish my thoughts of my mother. He told me what a wonderful woman she was: clever and beautiful and capable of huge love.

'I told him he was my papá. That I could never consider anyone else my father. He looked at me. He had tears in his eyes. He couldn't speak, he was so over-whelmed with emotion.

'That's when it happened. A tyre burst. You remem-ber how old that car was? We weren't travelling very fast, but when the tyre blew, my father wasn't looking at the road. He was looking at me. It all happened so fast. The car swerved, and although he tried, my father couldn't regain control. We veered into the ditch, then bounced out and spun. That's when we hit the tree.

'When we stopped, Papá was lying across the wheel, and his head was bleeding. I could smell petrol. I couldn't open the door, so I climbed out of the window. I ran to my father's door and started pulling at it, but it was stuck. The smell of petrol was strong, and I remembered Papá had been to the village when the last fuel delivery had been made. The car had nearly a full tank. Under the battered bonnet, I could see a flicker. I knew it was a flame.

'I realized I had to get my father out of the car. I was

screaming and shouting at him to wake up. After what seemed like an eternity, he lifted his head and turned to me. I shouted at him to open the door. He moved so slowly I was frantic. But he reached down to the handle on the inside, and as I pulled on the door, it flew open.

'Right at that moment, the front of the car burst into flames. Papá was too groggy to move, so I pulled him from the front seat and onto the road. I was still dragging him when the car exploded. The force blew both of us backwards. I hit my head and must have been unconscious for a while. I don't know how long it was, but when I woke up, Papá was on top of me.

'I wriggled out from under him, calling his name. But the moment I saw him, I knew he was dead. He had taken the brunt of the blast, and his body had shielded me. He was horribly burnt. I could barely look at him.

'I think I screamed. I remember calling for help – I don't know how long for. But the road was completely empty. We had been driving for hours, and I had no idea where we were or how I could get help.

'Then I realized no one could help my father now anyway. I sat down beside him and lifted his bloody head onto my lap. I put my arms around him and held his burnt body. I cried. I sobbed and I rocked his poor, broken body. I grieved for everything I had lost – all the family I would never know, and the one man who was truly my father.'

Alberto can see his father lying in his arms. He can feel his arms, stiff and sore. His father has been dead for some time. It's late and the sun is sinking in the sky. With one last kiss on his father's head, he stands and turns. He walks away from the road and into the bushes. He doesn't know where he's going, but he has to get away from this terrible scene.

Through the bushes and across the fields the child Alberto walks. He doesn't stop. The gorse scratches his legs, and he stumbles many times, but he keeps walking. The night becomes black and he can barely see his feet, but he keeps going.

His mind is a whirl. His father is dead. But he wasn't his father. Who is his father? Should he go home? It isn't his home anymore. Not now his father is dead. He has no mother and no father. He is an orphan.

He shakes his head as he walks, but the thoughts refuse to go away; instead, they shout at him, and the longer he walks, the more confused the thoughts become.

He finally stops for a moment and shuts his eyes. He takes himself inside his head. He sees his thoughts. They clatter and crash into each other. He realizes he doesn't want to think these thoughts anymore. He doesn't want to think about anything anymore. He screws his eyes very tight and looks at the thoughts. As he concentrates, the thoughts soften and swirl around his head. And then, quite purposefully, he sends them away. One by one, they disappear into a mist. His mind becomes blank. Now he doesn't know what to think, what to feel.

Suddenly, he hears talking. He realizes he is near a road and he creeps behind a bush and kneels down. He keeps very still. It is a group of men, soldiers, passing by. They are talking about food. He wonders if he is hungry but can't feel anything.

Waiting for the men to pass by, he is aware of leaves and twigs rubbing against his bare legs. He is just about to stand after the men have passed by when he hears more footsteps. He puts his head down and remains as still as he can.

Suddenly, something lands on his head. He senses more than feels his hair singeing and realizes it is a cigarette. Instinctively, he flicks it off his head. Then he holds his breath, staying as still as he can. He knows his life depends on it.

'Show yourself,' instructs a man's voice. He doesn't move. What should he do? His mind is blank. He does what he is told.

He clambers out of the bushes. He follows the orders and stands where he is instructed. With a sharp click, a flame lights up all their faces. He sees a pale man with freckles and a young man pointing a gun at him. They both wear black hats and dark uniforms.

'What's your name?' demands the pale man. The way he talks is strange. He doesn't sound the same as people Alberto knows.

'Alberto.'

'How did you get here?'

'I walked.'

'Where from?'

Thoughts try to return. They force against the thin

wall he has formed to keep them out. They push and push trying to get back in. *Where from?* they insist. *Where are you from? Who are you, and where are you from?*

With all the effort he can muster, Alberto pushes them out of his mind. He will not think of those things again. He will never let those thoughts back.

And suddenly the soldier is holding him. He realizes he is crying, and with a sense of relief, he collapses into the man's body.

When he has cried his fill, the pale man gives the young soldier an instruction. The young soldier takes his hand, and as he looks up, he sees the pale soldier smile, even in the dark. Obediently, he is led away.

After a short time walking, the young man says to him, 'Alberto, eh? What's your second name?'

'Romero.' He can say that without letting the thoughts back in, but he knows he can't say — can't remember — anything more or else the thoughts will return.

Then more questions. Where does he live? Where was he going? Where are his family? What was he doing walking in the dark?

He has a dim memory of a car, but he says nothing.

The memory skips and he is walking again. This time he is with the one they call El Rubio. They are walking in comfortable silence.

He listens to the quiet stamp of their footsteps and the swishing of the grass as it flicks past their legs.

He is enjoying each moment, concentrating on all of his senses and filling his mind with this peaceful moment.

'Alberto, are you sure you can't remember anything about your home?' the soldier asks.

He finds he cannot. He tries gently to see if there are any memories, but with relief, he realizes they have gone. Completely gone.

'No, nothing,' he says.

'Not even your mamá?'

Suddenly, he hears his own voice shout, *Mimi!* The memories bubble up again, but he stamps down on them, before they can grow.

The soldier pushes him with more questions. But he finds the more he is prodded for information, the more doors close in his mind. Everything is carefully locked away.

The soldier gives up and for a while they talk easily about his home in England, his strange accent and his sunshine-yellow hair. The Englishman tries to explain why he is fighting in the war. As he listens to talk of a battle for fairness against cruelty, he sees a boy push a girl over. He flies at the boy and hits him in the face.

He realizes he is standing still, and the soldier is talking to him. With reluctance he explains, 'I just had a memory.'

'What was it?'

'I hit another boy,' he replies.

'Why?'

He sees the boy push the girl again, but this time she

falls and falls and disappears into black. There's nothing there. The memory has gone.

'I don't know,' he says honestly.

The soldier is talking, but he isn't listening. For the first time, he is trying to remember. He tries to see the scene where he hit another boy. But it's not there. He tries to find something else in his memory – names, places, a home. But there's nothing there. He has dispelled them all. It's not quite as comforting as it should be.

Now the Englishman is talking about fighting and throws an easy punch at his shoulder. He punches the man half-heartedly in the leg. The soldier then shows him how to hit properly, how to hold his hand in a fist.

Remember this, he thinks then. Remember this moment with the Englishman – this is something to remember. This is a new memory.

Time skips by again. He is standing in a churchyard. A door is open, flooding light onto him and the soldier. They both stand in front of a priest. He is tall and bespectacled. The priest gives the Englishman a long look, turns to him, then back to the soldier.

In his long robes, the cleric steps forward and puts a hand on his head. He in turn looks to Rubio. After a moment, the man with the yellow hair smiles and winks at him. He relaxes. He is leaving one man he trusts and is in the care of another. He smiles at the Englishman before the priest leads him into the church.

The church feels safe and warm. The priest introduces himself as Father Francisco. Then, without speaking, the priest takes him to a tiny bedroom. There, he pulls back the covers on the bed, takes off the boy's jacket and boots, and helps him climb in. Then all is black.

When the sunlight reappears, he sees another soldier. This soldier is wearing an officer's khaki uniform. The officer and Father Francisco are having a discussion — it's very heated; they both seem angry. As he watches, the officer spits in the priest's face.

Fury rises in him and he sees himself running towards the soldier. He remembers Rubio's lesson in how to hit and curls his hand into a fist. With all his might, he punches the officer's leg. He is just about to hit him again when a hand flies towards him and strikes him across the face. He hurtles back and falls to the ground.

Father Francisco rushes to him and kneels down beside him. The officer storms away.

'Alberto,' says the priest, looking into his face, 'you shouldn't have done that. I understand why you did, but these are dangerous times. Take great care of becoming involved in other people's arguments. Captain García could have killed you — and just for the sake of a priest's pride.

'When you are older,' Francisco continues, 'you will

understand that there are times when you should get involved, and times when it is better to stand back.'

He watches the priest wipe the spit from his cheek with his sleeve.

'Why did he spit on you, Father?'

The priest looks at him and smiles. 'Because I am still learning when to stand back.'

The memory flitters and stutters forward in a staccato fashion, revealing emotions and images. He feels fear as he says goodbye to Father Francisco and climbs into a soldier's truck. He experiences an intense stab of grief as the truck passes fallen fighters and he sees the blond mop of El Rubio. He feels himself sink into a dark, deep hole and sees nothing. Then far away, he hears his name.

'Alberto,' says a woman's voice.

'Alberto.'

He blinks. He is holding a chunk of bread. The warm, sweet smell of chocolate wafts from it, and he is just about to take a bite when he hears his name again.

'Alberto.'

He looks up and sees a young woman. She is wearing an apron, and her dark hair is tied up — she has a serious look on her face. She holds a piece of paper in her hand. It is the piece of paper on which El Rubio wrote his name.

He smells the chocolate and feels the warm bread in his hand.

'Alberto.'

The old man looked up. Mimi sat in front of him. She held his hand tightly in hers.

'Alberto,' she said again softly.

Gruffly, he said, 'I saw it, Mimi. I saw it. Everything that happened. The memories are coming back.'

'It looks as if they are difficult memories,' said Mimi gently.

Alberto nodded.

Mimi put her hand on his arm. 'I'm so sorry,' she said quietly.

The old man looked at her and gave a sad smile. He lifted his glass of water to take a drink, but the glass shook with the trembling of his hand. Embarrassed, Alberto set the glass back down.

'Brandy?' asked Mimi.

Alberto smiled and nodded.

'Come with me,' said Mimi. 'I'll show you the collection and you can choose a brandy.'

Alberto raised his eyebrows at his friend.

'There is no one else I would rather share these wines with,' said Mimi.

Alberto smiled at her appreciatively.

Mimi led him out the back of the house to some stairs. At the bottom was a large oak door, which Mimi opened with a key.

'We had this cellar built for the collection,' she explained as she pushed the heavy door open, found a light switch and flicked it on.

The cool, stone room was lined with shelves, each filled with dusty bottles. Alberto breathed in the dry, musty air as he followed Mimi inside.

'The ones by the door are the more recent wines, including those sent by Javier. You see this marker here? This signifies the death of my father. To be honest, I'm not very interested in the wines after that. But here' — she waved her hand at the shelves of bottles — 'is the wine that my father and our ancestors before him made.'

Alberto peered at the bottles but was frightened to touch them, conscious of their value.

'There are more than five generations of our family's wines here. Some are better than others; some have not aged well. But there are some outstanding wines. My father was always very careful to maintain the collection, and I still have the log of all the wines stored here.'

'It must make you proud of your family,' said Alberto, taking in the scene.

'Yes,' said Mimi softly. 'Yes, it does. I'm still trying to decide what to do with the collection when I'm gone. My children don't want it — they don't have the historical links. And Néstor's children are even less interested than my brother.

'Of course, it's worth quite a lot of money. Maybe I should just sell the collection, even though the thought pains me, and split the profit in my inheritance. I know I have to make a decision soon, but I keep putting it off,' Mimi sighed.

Alberto nodded uncomfortably. He had barely anything to leave his children and grandchildren.

'Now,' said Mimi, brightening up and rubbing her hands together. 'The brandy collection is down here at the end.'

They crossed to the deepest part of the room, where the single bulb threw only a little light, and the shelves here were densely filled with the stout bottles.

'Our brandy became very popular locally,' explained Mimi. 'My father was always very proud of it, and the fact that he had expanded the business.' She reached up and brought down a bottle. She wiped the dust off the label and showed it to Alberto.

'This was a good year,' she said. 'My father really had a chance to develop the flavours. He and your father learnt a great deal from those first few years.'

'Did you say he and my father began the brandy production together?' asked Alberto thoughtfully. There was a memory fluttering around his mind.

'Yes,' said Mimi. She paused. She was remembering too: there was something significant about the beginning of the brandy production.

'Could we see an early bottle?' asked Alberto.

Mimi nodded and stepped to the corner of the room. There, she knelt down and wiped the tiny brass labels attached to the bottom shelf.

As she did, Alberto gasped. 'The first brandy,' he said. 'I remember our fathers talking about it. It was a celebration.'

'Yes,' said Mimi, turning to him. 'I remember too. The first bottle — it was dedicated to your mother!'

'And the label on the bottle . . .' said Alberto.

'. . . shows the years of her birth and her death. Oh, Alberto, she died on your birthday.'

Alberto nodded, suddenly unable to speak. He reached for the wall and placed his hand on the cool stones to steady himself. After all these years of not knowing, he was about to find his birthday.

Mimi reached for one of the bottles and slid it out of its shelf, then handed it to Alberto. Holding it carefully, he stepped towards the light. Mimi joined him, standing close beside him.

Alberto blew hard and a cloud of dust surrounded them. Then he wiped his hand over the label, revealing the Quintero family crest and, in heavy red letters beneath, the words QUINTERO BRANDY. As Alberto squinted at the faded ink, he saw words appear out of what he had first thought was a decorative flourish. It formed two dates.

At the sight of them, the old man smiled at the familiarity of his birthday.

Alberto turned to Mimi. 'Just wait until we tell the boy,' he said.

Chapter Sixteen

ANGELITA
16 April 1931

A sharp pain jabs me, making me gasp. But almost as soon as it comes, it is gone. I rub my back gently. Through the night, I had noticed aches, but I didn't wake Raúl. Instead, I had watched him sleep, his kind face relaxed. He is a fine man. Often I think he is too good for me. He has integrity and honour, characteristics I fear I lack.

I pour the warmed milk into the bowl of coffee and set it on the table. I pick at a sweet roll and lean against the table – the wood feeling cool on my legs through my smock.

'Good morning, my Angel,' says Raúl, walking into the small kitchen. He reaches out for my hand and kisses its palm.

I smile at him. I'm lucky. He treats me like a princess, not a fallen woman.

He sits down to his breakfast of sweet rolls with honey. Slurping his coffee, he indicates for me to sit with him. I ease my enormous body into the seat next to him.

'How are my wife and child today?' he asks warmly.

'We're fine. I felt a little pain earlier.' I see his eyebrows rise with a mixture of excitement and concern. 'I'm sure it's nothing,' I carry on hurriedly. 'The women say sometimes the body practises for what's to come. It doesn't mean the baby's coming yet.'

'But it's due soon, Angel. Should I call for the midwife?'

'No, Raúl. Not until we're sure. When you've gone to work, I'll go and see Chita.'

'All right. But you must send for me the moment anything happens.'

'Raúl,' I laugh, 'you know there's no point. What can you do except pace and fret? Better that you get on with your work and leave it to the women.'

'I can't bear the thought of you being in pain,' he says sadly.

'But think what the result will be,' I say, rubbing my huge stomach. As if to agree, the baby kicks.

Smiling, I reach for Raúl's hand and place it so he can feel the baby kicking. It's a sensation that Raúl never seems to tire of and he grins widely.

'It is a wonder,' he says, shaking his head.

'What?'

'The miracle of childbirth. The fact that any day a baby will arrive. A baby with ten perfect fingers and ten perfect toes. And, I'm sure, with your perfect beauty.'

There is a moment of discomfort as I wish I could return the compliment — tell him that I want the baby to have his calm and generous temperament. But I cannot.

Raúl sees my unease and, pushing his chair back, pulls me to him. Awkwardly, I sit on his lap, aware of my weight.

'Angelita, I know what you're thinking. Don't worry. This baby will be mine too. I will be there with you, bringing it up. It will be me teaching it to speak and count and read. It will learn my way of doing things. It may not have my nose, but it will have my sense of right and wrong. And I shall be proud of my achievements if it does.'

He rubs my back as I smile weakly at him. Usually it is me reassuring him, telling him that it is of little importance that he is not the baby's blood father. In the last few weeks, however, my mood has changed and I find myself full of doubts and fears.

'Don't be late for work,' I say, standing up and walking to the sink.

Raúl drains the last of his coffee and crosses over to me. He puts his arms around me and nuzzles into my neck.

'I love you, Angel,' he whispers.

I smile and, turning to him, kiss his lips, breathing in his soapy smell.

'I'll have lunch with Dante today,' he says as he heads for the door. 'Put your feet up and have some rest.'

I smile again at him as he leaves.

Washing the dishes, I look out of the window and think about that kiss. Every time I kiss Raúl, I wait for that feeling. That tiny sparkle inside me. The sensation of fairy dust sprinkled on my heart. I wait for it, but it never comes.

If I had not been in love before, I believe I would be happy with Raúl. He is warm and thoughtful, and he adores me. But I have been in love and I know what is missing.

I shake my head, trying to get rid of the thought. I do love Raúl. And he knows I do. But it is not a love that lights up like a fire inside and ignites a glow that cannot be extinguished.

Looking out of the window, my hands resting in the warm water, I think of that searing love. The sensation of pure happiness that surges through you every time you see the man you love. The knowledge that you must be together, that to be apart feels wrong and throws the world out of kilter. And when you are together, it is impossible not to touch him, to kiss him, to hold him. And to know absolutely that he feels the same way.

I shut my eyes and see his face. His eyes flecked with green. His soft brown curls. His strong chin. As I look at him, he says my name. *Angelita*. And he reaches both hands to cup my face and pulls me towards him to kiss him.

'Angelita?'

I turn quickly, flushed, to see Chita peeping in through the door.

'Come in, Chita,' I reply, wiping my hands on a cloth.

'Señor Raúl asked me to visit you,' says Chita, a smile on her face.

I am embarrassed. 'I'm sorry, Chita. You know how he worries. I'm sure it's nothing, just a little pain this morning.'

'You look well – you have a good colour. A little pain is to be expected at this time in your pregnancy. It may mean that the baby will come soon. Or it may not. It's up to the baby when it decides to come. Is it still moving?'

'Oh yes,' I say, laughing. 'It's been very active this morning.'

'Then everything is going well,' says Chita.

'Do you have time for some coffee?' I ask.

'Of course,' she says.

I know Chita works hard and I feel bad taking her from her chores, but I have few friends here. Everyone has been friendly and welcoming, but I know that some women feel uncomfortable with me. Sometimes they catch their men looking at me and become a little cold towards me.

Luckily, Dante and his wife both treat me as a long-lost sister. I feel at ease with Dante because, for all his cheeky comments, I know that he has no room in his heart for anyone other than his wife. Perhaps that's why he and Raúl get on so well – they are both content.

Chita has been important during my time here. She

has helped me learn to be a wife, to look after our home and my new husband. We have never spoken of it, but it's clear she knows that I never had to work in the home before. She is patient and kind to me, and I appreciate her friendship.

She tidies up a little while I make the coffee; then we sit at the table. It's an indulgent feeling. Usually at this time in the morning, we would be working through the day's chores.

'So,' says Chita, 'have you been thinking of names?'

'If it's a girl,' I reply, 'we will call her after my sister.'

'I didn't know you had a sister,' says Chita with interest.

'And if it's a boy,' I carry on quickly, 'we are still having discussions.'

Raúl and I have promised we won't speak of our family here. We agreed that we have started our lives anew. Our old lives are behind us.

But I miss my sister, Mercedes. She and I used to be so close. I know I am the one to have created a distance between us, but I wish we could return to the way things were. Maybe one day we'll go back and I can make amends.

'Discussions?' says Chita. 'It sounds as if you don't agree.'

'Raúl thinks a boy should be named after him — Raulito. If not, he likes Jesús.'

'Well, what's wrong with those names? It is tradition for your firstborn to take his father's name.'

'I think it's confusing to have two people in the same house with the same name. I know everyone does it, but I've always thought it was strange. But also, what if we have another boy? Won't he feel bad that he hasn't got his papá's name?'

Chita smiles. She clearly thinks I'm being ridiculous. 'And what is the reason for rejecting our good Lord's name?' she asks.

I sigh. I can't tell Chita that I have rejected not just his name, but the good Lord himself.

'There are just other names that I prefer.'

'Such as?'

'For most of my pregnancy, I've liked the name Eduardo,' I say. Chita nods approvingly. 'But,' I continue, 'lately I've been thinking about another name. I don't know where it came from – it just popped into my head one day.'

'What is it?'

'Alberto.'

'Alberto,' says Chita, trying it out. 'Yes, it's a good name. What does Raúl think?'

'He says when the baby comes, we'll know which name is right.'

'Well, he's correct,' says Chita.

Suddenly, the pain stabs again and I grasp the table. Chita reaches out and takes my hand.

'How long since the last pain?' she asks when I get my breath back.

'About twenty minutes.'

'And was this pain stronger than the last?'

'Yes, a bit. Has it started?' I ask nervously.

'Maybe,' she says, smiling and sitting back. 'I'll stay a while longer and we'll see what happens.'

I nod, feeling a little fluttering of fear in my stomach.

'Chita, will you do me a favour? Raúl is so anxious; I don't want him to be worried unnecessarily. Please don't tell him until the baby has arrived.'

Chita nods seriously. 'Unless,' she says, raising her finger at me, 'unless it is necessary to tell him.'

I realize she is suggesting that something may go wrong, and if my life is in danger, she will call him.

'Of course,' I agree cautiously.

'Perhaps,' says Chita, her face softening, 'you should have something else to eat. You need to keep your strength up.'

'I have some *magdalenas* in the pantry,' I smile, rising to fetch the plate of fluffy sponge cakes.

'I have noticed,' laughs Chita, 'that you only eat for two when it comes to cakes!'

I lean back into the pillow, panting hard. The last contraction was stronger than the others. Since my waters broke an hour ago, everything has changed.

Chita had immediately sent a boy to the town to fetch the midwife. Then she called for a girl to prepare lunch for the Quinteros and Raúl. When she had organized everything, she helped me into my nightdress and busied herself preparing the bed and collecting linen.

And now here I am, lying in the bed. I have been watching the clock to count the time between the pains. It is now only five minutes between each one.

There is a knock on the door and Chita opens it. A tiny lady dressed in black, her face creased with smile lines, enters the room.

'Hello, beautiful girl,' she greets me. 'Are you ready for the arrival of your precious little one?'

I nod, unable not to smile at this woman despite the pain.

'My name is María Teresa,' she says, handing a wicker basket to Chita.

'Señora?' I ask, confused. I cannot call someone so elderly whom I have never met before by their given name.

'Dear,' she says patiently, 'we are going to be intimately acquainted by the end of this. Let us be less formal from the beginning.'

'Oh,' I say uneasily.

Chita takes her to the kitchen, where I hear them murmuring quietly.

When they return, María Teresa is wearing an apron and has her sleeves rolled up. 'Shall we see where we are, dear?' she asks.

I nod and let her examine me.

'Ooh,' she says with delight. 'All's going well. It

shouldn't be too much longer now, and then you'll have your special little gift.'

I feel myself relax a tiny amount. But the moment is brief and I feel another wave of pain coming fast.

'Now, dear,' says the old woman, grasping my hand, 'breathe. That's it. Breathe. And think of something lovely.'

I squint at her in disbelief.

'Yes, yes,' she nods gleefully. 'Close your eyes and think of something, or someone, that makes you happy.'

I try, but all I can think of is the pain. When it is over, María Teresa pushes my hair away from my damp face and says, 'I know it's difficult, dear, but it will help. Think of a place where you feel relaxed. Or perhaps being with your husband. Or a food that you adore. If you can think of that, and not the pain, it will bring you some relief.'

'I'll try,' I say.

'Very good,' says María Teresa brightly as she bustles into the kitchen.

Chita returns with a bowl of water. Sitting beside me, she sets the bowl on the side table and dips a cloth in it. After wringing it out, she lays the cool cloth on my forehead.

'Thank you, Chita,' I smile at her.

Chita looks sadly at me and says, 'I'm sorry that your mother cannot be here with you. This is a time to be with your daughter.'

I haven't thought of my mother in weeks. We were

never close, but it has been easier than I expected to dispel her from my thoughts. I know Raúl misses his family a great deal, but apart from Mercedes, I do not.

The thought of my mother in this room fills me with horror. Oh no, the last thing I would want right now is my mother by my bedside. Warmth and support do not come naturally to her. She would certainly not approve of the cheery midwife — serious things must be conducted seriously in her opinion.

If my mother knew of my affair, and of this baby, I truly don't know what she would do. Perhaps she would shun me instantly. Turn her back on me and refuse to let any member of my family ever speak to me again. Or she might insist that we tell everyone that the baby was born early, yet remind me regularly that my child is a bastard. And she would insist a child born of sin was instantly baptized to save it from the flames of hell.

It will be difficult enough for me to dissuade Raúl from baptizing the baby. In the past few months, I have been considering this. While I have my opinion about the Church and religion, is it my place to impose it on a baby? My resolution has been that when it is old enough, we must let the child decide independently. I shall have problems explaining this to Raúl, though, I know, as he is more religious than even he realizes.

It is most likely that the child will be influenced by the Catholic society all around us, and want to be a part of it as opposed to excluded from it. And if that's enough, to feel part of something, then so be it. I'll be happy to support that decision. But I shall never return to the Church. It has caused me too much pain, and shown me it is an institution of suffering, not love. It repels me with its oppression and cruelty. As I think of what the Church has done to me, I feel a rage stir within me.

'Another one?' asks Chita, gently patting my head with the cloth.

I realize that the pain is returning and I nod.

María Teresa told me to think of something that makes me happy. I close my eyes tight and think of Raúl. I see his smiling face. I feel nothing but the pain. I try again and remember a day a few months ago when Raúl and I went out in the car. We took a picnic to a field full of wild lavender and we lay in the sun and the scent-filled air.

But still the pain is unbearable. In desperation, I think of the face that I only rarely allow myself to see. He appears in front of me. His earnest look breaks into an easy smile and I see him chuckle. There is a light in his eyes that makes his face glow and I feel myself smile back at him.

'Well,' exclaims María Teresa, 'whatever you're thinking of is working, isn't it?'

Puffing through the fading pain, I nod at the old woman and hope that she doesn't ask me what I'm thinking of.

And so it continues. The pain comes and I think of my lover and the thought of him eases the pain.

Over the hours, I think of the time we spent together. I remember when we first met. The fragrance of incense, the murmuring of the congregation and that handsome face as he leant towards me. It was clear we both felt something when we looked on one another for the first time. He stumbled over his blessing and I nearly choked on the host. Then our new priest smiled the tiniest of smiles at me and I knew I had to see that smile again.

As the pain rushes in again, I recall our first kiss. I had asked him to hear my confession, and confessed my feelings for him. He told me to pray for the Almighty's forgiveness. Then, because it was late, he offered to walk me home. As we crossed the dark, empty park, I stopped and tried to kiss him. At first, he pushed me away, but then, as we looked into each other's eyes, he pulled me to him and kissed me passionately.

The next time the pain comes, I remember our first night together. In his small, musty-smelling room, we hid under the covers. He held me tight and we whispered our love. We were so comfortable with one another, it was as if we had known each other all our lives. Without his robes, he was a man like any other. And yet a man unlike any other I had met.

And then, when there seems to be no respite from the pain, María Teresa tells me to push. As I do, I imagine it is not Chita holding my hand, but Antonio. It is Antonio who whispers in my ear that the baby's head is appearing. His warm voice telling me that I must keep bearing down. I squeeze his hand tightly and scream while he tells me I'm doing well and our baby is nearly with us. When I think I can bear it no longer, I hear Antonio say that our boy has arrived, and it is over.

Chita wraps the bloody bundle in soft cloths, then lifts it towards me. I see the tiny baby screw up his face and release a cry that to me sounds like music. I feel such an incredible surge of love for this tiny being that I can barely breathe. I hold him gently and his warm head falls on my chest.

'It's a boy,' says Chita, wiping my forehead.

'I know,' I say, gazing into my child's face. 'His name is Alberto.'

Chita smiles at me kindly until María Teresa nudges her and whispers urgently.

Ignoring them, I continue to look at my baby, drinking in his face, his tiny tuft of sticky hair, his wrinkled fingers.

I am vaguely aware of Chita quickly leaving the room and returning with fresh towels and sheets. I see her gather bloodstained sheets and rush out of the room with them. I hear the door open and Chita calls for a boy. I hear her speak quickly and quietly to whoever comes before closing the door again.

For a tiny moment, I break my gaze from my beautiful baby to look at María Teresa. Her face is worried and stern. She sees me looking at her and instantly a smile lights her face.

'Nothing to worry about, lovely. There's just a bit

too much blood. Chita has sent for the doctor, but I'm sure everything will be fine. You enjoy your gorgeous boy.'

My gorgeous boy squeezes his eyes shut and shakes his head. I sense the figure of Antonio by my side, and the faint scent of incense.

'Welcome, Alberto,' I say quietly to him. 'Your father and I are so pleased you're here.'

Chita comes back to me, a worried look on her face. It snaps me back to reality. Of course I know that Antonio is not here. And the expression on Chita's face makes me say to her, 'Please tell Raúl.'

She nods and dashes out of the room. I hear the door slam and turn back to Alberto, who squirms in his swaddling cloths. 'Albertino,' I whisper to him, 'you must know that you were born out of the truest of loves. Whatever happens, I will always be with you.'

I realize that tears are streaming down my face. The pain is returning, but this time it is too much and I cannot divert my mind from it.

Chita returns to my side, and she speaks. But it's as if she is speaking from a very long distance and I have to strain to hear her. She says that Raúl is outside and the doctor is on his way. I suddenly feel very drowsy and struggle to keep my eyes open. As I strain to look at Alberto, he is gently taken from my arms. I want to object. I want to cry, *No — don't take my baby!* but the desire to sleep is too strong and I succumb.

As I drift away, I see Antonio. I reach out to touch him, but then I see an anxious look on his gaunt face. Looking around, I see Raúl is beside me, smiling. My mother and father stand just behind me. With a sinking feeling I realize what I see is my wedding day.

The man I am in love with, the love of my life, stands before me, reading the scripture. The man that I love, who told me that our love could not be, that it was impossible for us to be together, that what had happened between us was a mortal sin. The man that I love, who chose God above me.

I remember him telling me it was over. All of my pleading and wailing had come to nothing. He had stood firm, pale and miserable, and insisted that God was his one true love.

A short time later, when I discovered I was expecting Antonio's child, I considered telling him. But his words had been so final, I didn't dare try even to speak to him again. In my distress and loneliness, I had turned to an old friend. Raúl had suggested what seemed to be the answer to all our problems. Fear drove me to agree and feign delight when we announced our engagement to our parents.

Just a few short weeks later, I entered the chapel on my wedding day, dressed in my mother's white dress, the long veil hiding my wretchedness. And as I turned from a grinning Raúl to the priest, I saw Antonio. It had never crossed my mind to ask who my father would appoint to conduct the ceremony. The horror of the situation overwhelmed me and I fainted. Raúl caught me, while Antonio looked on, his pain obvious.

My mother's smelling salts and stern words made me compose myself and the marriage continued. I could barely look at either Antonio or Raúl. And when the ceremony was over, I swore I would never step foot in another church. A God that creates such intense love, then forbids it, then throws it back in your face, is not a God that I want to worship.

For a moment, I see Antonio's face again. My heavy veil masks his features, but I see his warm eyes swimming with tears. The sight makes me sigh with sorrow and weariness.

'Angelita,' says an insistent voice.

Stirring, I try to open my eyes, but I am too tired.

'Angelita,' says the voice, louder this time.

I force my eyes open and see the doctor. He is holding my wrist and looking at his watch. I notice María Teresa standing over me, rubbing my stomach. There are no smiles now; her face is stern and set. Behind her, I see Chita standing in the doorway holding a small bundle. I relax, knowing my baby is nearby.

I want to speak to the doctor, ask what is happening, but I don't have the strength. Far away, I hear a splashing sound and see María Teresa look down with a horrified expression on her face. The doctor drops my arm and steps towards my legs. As I look up, I see Chita disappear out of the door.

Everything is swimming now. I see Raúl, his worried

face looking down at me, speaking words I cannot hear. I see Mercedes as a child, laughing as we chase each other across the garden, our white Communion dresses fluttering in the wind. I see Antonio, his handsome face breaking into a large smile as he says my name over and over. And then I see a small boy, with soft brown curls and eyes flecked with green. He looks at me seriously, but as I smile at him, I see the tiniest of smiles turn the corners of his lips.

I think he is the most beautiful child I have ever seen.

Chapter Seventeen

16 April 2006

Albertino stood on his tiptoes and reached up to the fattest lemon he could see. The leaves rustled as he twisted and broke the stalk. Carefully, he lifted the lemon to his nose and breathed in, as he had seen his grandfather do so many times.

The lemon smelt fresh and sweet and clean, and he nodded to himself before turning and bounding off to the table with it. There, Señora Ortiz was making up jugs of sangria. The boy handed the large lemon to her and she smiled at him.

'That's a big one,' she said, squeezing it. 'Thank you, Tino.' She picked up a large knife and cut the lemon in half.

Beside her, other women from the village were opening bottles of wine and lemonade, and breaking large blocks of ice wrapped up in towels. Albertino wondered if Papá would let him try a little sangria today.

He looked towards his parents. They were standing together talking to his aunt and uncle. His papá looked healthy and well, despite leaning on a walking stick. His mother smiled and rubbed her husband's back gently as she listened to her sister talk.

When he had returned home after his trip with his grandfather, Albertino had been wary of going to the hospital for the first time. But instead of the silent, frightening Egyptian mummy, his father had been sitting up and talking. He still had some bandages on his head, but his face had been uncovered. Although swollen and discoloured, it was Papá.

On that first visit, his mamá had allowed him to sit very carefully on the edge of the bed and talk to his papá. His father listened with interest to Tino's account of their search for Apu's birthday, occasionally asking questions about who they had met, and what they had discovered.

Albertino had noticed that his father kept his hands under the covers. The boy's mother had told him Papá's hands were going to take a long time to recover. And she was right. His father had been through many operations as the surgeons tried to make his hands and arms better.

Rosa had explained to her son that the doctors had taken some skin from other parts of Papá's body and put it on the part that was burnt the worst. She said that the skin started to grow just like it was always supposed to be there, and soon it would look like new. These days, all these months on, Albertino thought his papá's hands looked much better than they did, but they still didn't look like before. His father's fine and dexterous fingers were now fat and clumsy. He watched his father struggle to do things that he used to do without thinking – Mamá even had to cut up his food for him like a baby.

His papá hadn't worked since the accident. His mother had taken more shifts at the factory, but the boy had heard his parents talk in hushed tones when they thought he wasn't listening, and he knew they were worried about money.

But today, it seemed that they had put their worries aside. Albertino thought his mother looked pretty in her best dress and his father very smart in his hat. He had to wear a hat all the time he was outside now, as his skin was sensitive to the sun, but his father said he would start a fashion for men's wide-brimmed hats that would spread across the country.

'So, little one,' said Señora Ortiz, 'would you like to see who wants sangria?'

The boy nodded and carefully picked up a large earthenware jug, filled to the brim with the crimson liquid, slices of lemon and orange bobbing on the surface with the ice. Gingerly walking across the dried earth, he made his way towards a group of men. Tall and cheery, Andrés stood at the centre of them. The group were mainly men from the village, but after so many years looking after customers in Los Niños, Andrés was comfortable chatting with strangers.

Seeing the boy approach with the full sangria jug, Andrés stepped forward to help.

'Is this for us, Tino?' he asked.

When the boy nodded shyly, Andrés took the jug from him, saying, 'Let me — I'm a professional, you know.'

'Señores?' he said, holding the jug up to them.

Most of the men nodded happily and lifted their glasses. As he began to fill the mixture of plastic cups, wine glasses and mugs, Andrés began to sing.

'*And I say thank you to the Señor for the women. Yes, the women and the wine . . .*'

His voice was strong and melodic, and while some of the men joined in, others sipped their drinks and listened, smiling at the familiarity of the old song.

The boy smiled too as he watched Andrés raise his glass to the heavens and thank the Lord one last time for the sangria. The men cheered with approval as he finished the song, and those standing around clapped appreciatively.

As Andrés started to sing another song, Albertino dashed over to his parents. His aunt and uncle had moved on to talk to some family friends, and his mother was talking quietly to his father.

'Mamá, Papá,' cried the boy, running up, 'Señor Andrés is singing!'

'Oh,' said his mother. 'So he is. He's very good, isn't he?'

'Yes,' replied his father, nodding. 'Remind me,' he asked — although he already knew the answer — 'where did you and Apu meet him?'

'At Los Niños – the restaurant. His mamá is Doña Isabel. She looked after Apu when he was in the orphanage,' said the boy excitedly.

'Ah, that's right. If he sings like that in his restaurant, maybe we should take a day out and go for lunch.'

Albertino nodded enthusiastically, but his mother said softly, 'Remember, Juan Carlos, we have to be careful with our money.'

'Pah,' said Juan Carlos. 'I'll be working again in no time and we'll have days out as often as we want.'

The boy noticed his mother's fleeting glance at his papá's scarred hands leaning on his walking stick before smiling at her husband.

Suddenly, they heard the squealing of children, accompanied by the excited barking of a dog. Albertino looked towards the sound of the fun and grinned. His friends from school were playing with his cousins from the city. In the middle of the group was Bonita, his dog.

A few months after his father had come home from hospital, the family had gone to the local pound. There, his parents had let him choose a dog, although they guided him away from the dogs that were too big for their apartment and the puppies that were too little to be away from their mothers.

In the end, they had all fallen in love with a scruffy little bitch. Her dirty grey hair was matted, and she could barely see out of her gummed-up eyes. They had taken her straight to Rosa's friend who had a dog-grooming parlour and left the dog in her hands, returning an hour later to find a dog they didn't recognize. Her white fur was cropped short, even around her long, elegant tail and dainty feet, and her large dark eyes glowed with happiness.

As everyone gushed at the prettiness of the dog, her name had been decided. 'She is Bonita,' announced the boy proudly. Bonita quickly settled into the family home and Albertino took her for a long walk every day after school. The dog slept at the foot of his bed at night, and Juan Carlos told him she sat by the door for half an hour before he came home from school.

Now she was barking excitedly as the children chased each other round the trees on the terraces. Thrilled at the thought of joining the game, Albertino was about to dash off towards them when he heard a familiar voice behind him.

'Good afternoon, Tino.'

The boy turned and saw Father Samuel approaching, smiling broadly.

'Hello, Father,' he replied.

'What a beautiful day for your grandfather's birthday party,' said the priest, holding out his hands and looking up to the spotlessly blue sky.

'Father,' said the boy's mother, holding out her hand to shake his and giving a respectful bob of her head. 'Thank you for coming. We're all so glad you could make it.'

'Thank you for the invitation,' said Father Samuel, shaking her hand graciously. 'You must be Albertino's parents.'

'Yes, this is my husband, Juan Carlos.'

The priest turned to the boy's father, his hand outstretched. But Juan Carlos's hands remained resting on his walking stick, and after a brief glance at them, misshapen hands, the priest gently grasped the man's arm.

'Father,' Juan Carlos nodded at the priest.

'My apologies,' said Father Samuel. 'Doña Isabel told me of the accident. How is your recovery progressing?'

'Very well, thank you, Father,' replied Juan Carlos.

'I'm sure it has not been easy,' said the priest sincerely.

'No, Father, you're right,' said Rosa. 'But Juan Carlos has been very brave. All through the operations and therapy he has remained cheerful.'

'Excellent!' said the priest. 'Sometimes God sends us challenges and demands a great deal from us. It has always been my opinion that a positive attitude in the face of adversity is an asset.'

Juan Carlos nodded seriously. 'It's true what they say, Father, that being faced with death makes one appreciate life. Now I see things I may have missed before. And we are both determined not to waste our precious days.' He smiled at Rosa warmly.

'We should all count our blessings every day,' nodded Father Samuel. 'And may I add,' he continued, turning to Albertino, 'how sorry I was to hear the sad news of your grandfather. You must miss him very much,' he said gently.

The boy's breath caught as it always did when he remembered Apu was gone. Hot tears welled in his eyes as the image of his grandfather on that awful evening flashed in front of him.

Apu had come to his house for the evening. Albertino's father had only been home from the hospital for a few weeks, and was in bed. His mother had prepared *fideuà* – Apu's favourite, saffron-coloured noodles with lumps of fish and seafood nestled in its thick stock sauce. His grandfather told him it was what the fishermen cooked when they were out at sea, and it came from the part of Spain where they lived.

The three of them chatted, sopping up the rich, fishy juices with chunks of bread.

'And we should have fireworks for your birthday, Apu.'

The old man waved his hand, brushing away the idea.

'He's right, Papá,' his mother said. 'All those years you didn't have a birthday to celebrate – we should make this a real fiesta.'

'No, no. I don't want a fuss.'

'I do!' Tino declared.

His mother smiled, and as his grandfather looked at him, he slowly nodded. He spoke quietly. 'Maybe just a few fireworks. Let's see what my pension can afford.'

'Well,' his mamá said, 'we have plenty of time to save up for it. And we clearly have a lot to plan.'

Albertino nodded forcefully. He was taking full responsibility for Apu's first birthday party. Aunt Mimi had said there had been celebrations for his birthday when he was a very young boy, but that was a whole lifetime ago. In a few months' time, he would have the best fiesta ever.

'Thank you, Rosa,' Alberto said, pushing away his empty plate.

'My pleasure, Papá,' his daughter replied, standing and crossing to the oven. She opened the door and took out the warming plate of food with a cloth. As she placed it on a waiting tray, she suggested, 'Tino, why don't you and Apu watch some television while I take Papá his meal?'

'Apu,' he said excitedly, 'maybe *Los Simpsons* will be on.'

His grandfather settled into the armchair in front of the television as the boy chattered away about his favourite show. But the evening news was on, so he picked up his toy car and drove it over the furniture, humming the noise of the engine.

'Albertino,' his grandfather said quietly.

'Yes?' he replied, driving the car up the leg of Apu's chair.

'I'd like to thank you,' the old man said gruffly.

The child stopped making the engine noise and, kneeling in front of him, looked at his grandfather. 'What for?'

Alberto took a deep breath and continued, 'Thank you for making me search for my birthday. I never expected to find it. But I did. And I found old friends. And memories that I thought had gone forever.'

He leant over and held his grandson's face in his large, leathery hand. 'And I would never have had that joy without you.'

The boy smiled up at his grandfather. Compliments from Apu were rare and he was pleased to receive these kind words.

'You're a very special boy. And I believe you will be a special man. Remember that. Your apu believes you will do wonderful things in your life.'

He placed a soft kiss on his grandson's forehead and smiled at him with tears in his eyes. Albertino smiled back, proud of his grandfather's words.

Then Apu's eyes narrowed and he rubbed his chest with his hand.

'Apu?'

His grandfather winced and, breathing out heavily, said to his grandson, 'I'm fine. Get me a brandy, will you?'

The boy dashed off into the kitchen, where he carefully took the bottle — the brandy his mamá kept especially for Apu — out of the cupboard and slowly measured out two fingers of the amber liquid as his grandfather had shown him many times.

When he had returned to the lounge, he'd seen Apu

slumped forward, clutching his arm and letting out a grumbling groan.

'Mamá!' the boy shouted as he stood, rooted to the spot.

His mother came dashing into the room and, as soon as she saw her father leaning over in agony, rushed to his side.

'Papá!' she'd cried, as Tino edged towards them both, still holding the brandy.

'Sit with Apu,' his mother said to him loudly as she stood up and pushed past him.

Obediently, Tino sat on the floor beside his grandfather, placing the glass of brandy beside him. Looking up, he took in Apu's red, strained face, the muscles in his neck taut, veins throbbing visibly.

'Apu?' he said in a scared voice.

But his grandfather didn't reply.

The boy had heard his mother speak into the phone. Her father was having a heart attack, he had heard her say. She told whoever was on the other end to hurry. Please come quickly, she pleaded before slamming down the phone.

Then she had rejoined her son, sitting on the other side of Apu. As they watched, they saw his face start to relax. The muscles and veins softened, released of their intense strain, and his body slowly eased back into the chair. As it did, Apu gave a long, heavy sigh.

'Papá?' Rosa cried, shaking his arm violently.

But Apu had lain back, his face slack, his mouth open. As his mother frantically felt around her father's neck for a pulse, the boy looked at his grandfather's face. To Tino, Apu looked like he did when he dozed off in front of the television. He looked as though he were sleeping peacefully.

The ambulance had arrived not long after, and two men in uniforms rushed into the house. They quickly but gently pulled Apu onto the floor. Tino saw one of them knock over the glass of brandy, spilling his grandfather's drink on the floor. No one else noticed. While one of the medics pumped Apu's chest with his hands, the other opened a small case with what looked like a little machine in it.

'Tino!' his mother said sternly to him.

He wrenched his eyes away from the men leaning over his grandfather and looked at his mother, who was kneeling on the floor by Apu's head.

'Go to your papá,' she said. 'Now!'

He had wanted to stay and watch, but the tone of his mother's voice told him not to argue. He ran into his father's room, where his papá, worried, asked what was going on. Tino had explained as well as he could about the ambulance men, and about the machine, and that Apu just looked like he was asleep.

His father had lifted his bandaged hands up and opened his arms. Tino fell into his papá's body and his father hugged him tightly.

'Maybe he's just asleep, Papá,' he had said, as he

fought back the scary feeling that fluttered in his stomach.

His father hadn't said anything, just held him. Perhaps it was then that Tino had realized that Apu was not sleeping.

But now, all these months on, he liked to think that he'd been right the first time, and that's what dying was like. It was like going to sleep, forever. Apu was having a lovely siesta — and was able to watch over his family in his dreams.

Rosa looked at her son, blinking away his tears, and placing a reassuring hand on his shoulder, said, 'Thank you, Father,' to the priest.

'Did your grandfather ever tell you what he did at my church?' asked Father Samuel with a wry smile.

The boy shook his head, swallowing hard.

'Well,' said the priest as Rosa and Juan Carlos leant in to hear the story, 'do you remember you got a bit dirty when you were climbing the tree and I took you into the church to clean up?'

The boy nodded seriously.

'Your grandfather and I had been talking about someone who was buried in the church graveyard. The burial had taken place a very long time ago, but the grave didn't have a headstone. It just had a simple wooden cross to mark the place. There wasn't even a name on the cross.

'I had been trying to get a headstone for the grave, but as I told your grandfather, things do not happen swiftly in an institution as large as the Church. Rightly, your grandfather considered this a poor excuse and took matters into his own hands.

'When you had gone, I went back into the church-yard. There, I found that your grandfather had carved the man's name into the wooden cross.' He looked at Rosa and Juan Carlos and smiled. 'Such a simple action, but it says a great deal about the compassion of Alberto.'

'What was his name?' asked the boy. 'The man who was buried?'

'Antonio,' replied the priest, 'Father Antonio.'

'A priest?' asked Rosa, surprised. 'How strange.'

Father Samuel nodded at her before continuing, 'I have taken a leaf out of your grandfather's book, Tino. In commemoration of your grandfather, I have had a headstone built for the grave. It will arrive and be placed next week. And I intend to say a few words — a blessing for the soul who is buried there.'

'What does it say?' asked Albertino. 'The head-stone?'

'It's very simple. I didn't have any details other than a name. So it just says, "Father Antonio. Commended to God. May he rest in peace."'

'That's very kind of you,' smiled Rosa. 'I wish my father could have known of your actions.'

'He knows,' said the boy clearly. When the three adults turned to him, he said confidently, 'Apu is always with us. You said so, Mamá. And now he knows about the gravestone.'

Smiling, Juan Carlos reached across to his son and gently ruffled his hair with his thick-fingered hand.

'Father,' said Rosa, 'can I offer you something to eat? The whole village is here and everyone's brought something. We too could feed the five thousand, there's so much food.'

Grinning, Father Samuel let himself be led towards the trestle tables laden with food.

'Papá?' said the boy, looking up at his father.

'Yes?'

'Apu *is* here with us, isn't he?'

His father nodded. 'Yes. He is. He will always be with you and your mamá. And he will always be here on this land.'

Together, they looked across the small plot. The almond and lemon trees, the vines and the tiny corner of flowers. And now the patch of land was filled with people who had come to Alberto's birthday party.

Rosa had made copies of Albertino's hand-drawn poster and they had pinned the party invitation all over the village. She had also tracked down people the boy and his grandfather had met on their search for his birthday. And, as Señora Ortiz had predicted all that time ago, the whole village had come out for the occasion. Albertino was proud that Apu was such a well-liked person.

While the women had covered plates in strips of sliced hams and chorizo, and prepared two large paellas to cook outdoors, the men had brought beers and wines — many home-made. The butcher had donated a whole pig — it was so big that the baker had cooked it in his oven. And Rosa and her sisters had ordered a huge birthday cake edged with nuts, Alberto's name spelt out in blue icing.

Albertino wished his grandfather could be here to appreciate it. Even if he was watching from heaven, it wasn't the same as being here. He imagined Apu standing with him, embarrassed about the fuss, but secretly pleased to see so many friends and neighbours mixing happily with his family.

The boy's memory was broken by a frenzy of barking. Turning quickly, he saw Bonita fly past him, yapping madly. And there, tearing towards her and yelping delightedly in return, was Vito. The two dogs met joyously, bouncing noisily around each other.

Grinning, the boy looked past the two dogs and saw Mimi walking towards him.

'Aunt Mimi,' cried Albertino, running towards her.

When she saw him, Mimi opened her arms. He ran into them and she hugged him hard.

Rosa and Juan Carlos approached, smiling.

'Thank you so much for coming, Mimi,' said Rosa.

'It's my pleasure,' replied Mimi, hugging her gently. 'How are you, Juan Carlos?' she asked as he limped towards them.

'Much better than the last time you saw me,' he grinned.

'Yes, you look much better than at the funeral, especially your walking,' she commented.

'It's the exercises I make him do,' teased Rosa.

'She's a tough boss,' grinned Juan Carlos, putting an arm around his wife, 'but I know all the hard work is paying off.'

'And your hands?' asked Mimi gently.

'Oh, you know,' replied Juan Carlos, lifting up one of his ugly hands to show her. 'Little by little.'

Mimi nodded sympathetically.

At that moment, Vito and Bonita ran up to them, jumping and slathering over them all.

Laughing, Albertino knelt down to their level and let them lick and nudge him. As he played with the two dogs, it was impossible to tell which of the three was happiest.

Leaning over the giggling child, Mimi handed Rosa a bag. It clinked loudly and she said, 'Just a few bottles. Not the best stuff, but perfectly good for sangria.'

Rosa kissed Mimi's cheek as she thanked her and delivered the bottles to Señora Ortiz.

'What a wonderful party!' Mimi said to Juan Carlos.

Across the stretch of land, children played noisily, a group of men sang, old women dressed in black and sitting on folding chairs gossiped loudly, and other people milled around the tables filled with plates of food and paella dishes.

'He was a very popular man.'

Mimi nodded. 'He was a wonderful friend when we

were children,' she said sadly. 'I just wished I'd been able to spend time with him once we'd found each other again.'

'Rosa says he came back from that trip a different man. He had always been content with what he had, but she said it was as if he'd received a gift he'd never expected. And it was the best gift he could have wished for,' said Juan Carlos.

'I wish Rosa could have seen his face when he saw that bottle with the date of his birth on it. And, of course, as soon as he saw the date, he remembered it. He remembered the birthday parties we'd thrown him, and gifts his father had given him. He became quite emotional.'

'He was not a man who often showed his emotions.'

'May I ask what happened to the bottle of brandy?' asked Mimi.

'It's Tino's now,' replied Juan Carlos. 'It was his idea to search for his grandfather's birthday, so we all agreed he should have it. His mother and I will look after it for him until he's ready to take it. I don't know whether he will drink it or keep it somewhere safe; he's a bit young to think of things like that now.'

'When the time comes, he'll make the right decision,' said Mimi. They both watched the child racing the dogs in circles. 'He's a wonderful child.'

'Thank you,' smiled Juan Carlos. 'Now, can I help you to a drink?'

Just then, the dogs barrelled past them, nearly knocking Juan Carlos off his feet.

'Tino!' cried Mimi. 'Don't excite those dogs any more than they already are!'

The boy grinned at Mimi and dashed after the barking dogs, who were heading for a group of people sitting chatting.

'Tino! There you are,' said a familiar voice.

The boy turned and saw among those seated an elderly woman with short white hair and glasses.

'Doña Isabel,' he said happily. Then the boy realized that sitting on either side of her were the gardener and his wife from Los Zorros.

They greeted him happily with kisses and smiles.

'You were playing when we arrived,' explained the gardener. 'I recognized Doña Isabel straight away and we have been catching up on old times.'

'See what you and your grandfather have done?' asked Isabel. 'You've brought together old friends. It's wonderful — I'm so pleased to have someone to talk to about the old days.'

'We do have some sad news, though,' said the gardener.

The boy turned to him, a worried look on his face.

'It's not such bad news,' smirked his wife. 'Old General García passed away last month.'

'Oh,' said the boy. He knew he should act as if this was very sad news, but he could not bring himself to do so, so he kept quiet.

'So what's happened to the old orphanage now?' asked Isabel.

'The government has bought the building,' said the gardener. 'It's not definite, but we believe they are planning to turn it into a care home for the elderly. We have already been approached about continuing to work there.'

'I was hoping they would turn the building into housing for immigrants,' chortled his wife. 'That evil old man would be rolling in his grave if they had!'

The boy smiled. He didn't know what an immigrant was, but anything that made the wizened, nasty man — the man who had been so horrid to Apu — spin in his grave seemed like a good thing to him.

Later in the evening, Albertino's uncles hung lanterns from the trees. A wind had picked up, and both the lanterns and the nearby rosemary bushes rustled in the breeze. The women wrapped their shawls tightly around them against the chill. Tired children dozed on their parents' laps, while the men continued to drink and sing and laugh.

The boy had been playing with his cousins and the other children when he saw Vito trotting back towards Mimi. Bonita followed her friend, and he, in turn, followed his dog.

Mimi was talking quietly with his parents, each of them nursing a glass of wine.

'No,' he heard his father say as he approached. 'It's not right.'

'I agree,' said his mother. 'It's too much, Mimi.'

'What's too much?' asked the boy.

The three adults fell silent in the flickering light.

Mimi was the first to speak. 'I have decided I would like to give your parents a gift. It will help them while your father can't work, but it is also a gift to you – for your future.'

'What is it?' asked Albertino.

'My collection of wine,' replied Mimi.

'I don't like wine,' said the boy.

Despite himself, his father laughed. 'It's not for drinking,' he said.

'What's it for, then?'

'Such a large collection of special wines and brandies is worth a lot of money,' explained his mother.

'It's far too valuable a gift,' said his father firmly.

'Listen to me,' said Mimi. 'If it weren't for a stupid mistake my brother made, I believe Alberto would have stayed on and worked at Quintero's. I think he would have spent the rest of his life on the vineyard. It was a big part of his life as a child and it would have been a part of his future.'

'But what happened all those years ago, happened,' said Rosa. 'You owe us nothing now.'

'I know I don't,' said Mimi, sighing. 'But Tino brought Alberto back to me. He gave me a friend I thought I had lost forever. All the money in the world couldn't have done that. But a small boy with a big heart could. And now I'd like to do something for him. Please,' she said simply, 'let me do this.'

'But it should go to your family,' said Juan Carlos.

'My family don't need it,' Mimi said firmly. 'Their father left me plenty of money, and I shall leave them that when I die. And, sad though it is, they're not interested in the history of the collection.'

'I don't know,' said Juan Carlos.

'Consider it not as a gift from me, but a gift from Alberto. I had decided to give him the collection after he left. I was planning to arrange it immediately and would have told him when I next saw him. But I never got the chance.'

'Really?' asked Rosa.

'Really,' said Mimi. 'And I can't believe Alberto would have done anything else but pass it on to the grandson who helped him find his birthday. Can you?'

The boy watched his mother and father as they looked at each other, unspoken words passing between them. Slowly, Juan Carlos nodded to Rosa.

The boy's mother turned to Mimi and smiled. Mimi smiled back and the women hugged.

Then it was Juan Carlos's turn to hug the elderly woman. He wiped tears from his eyes and said, 'I don't know what to say.'

'Why don't we raise a glass to Alberto?' said Mimi.

Albertino watched as the three of them silently lifted their glasses to the sky.

Suddenly, a whistle rang out and a light shot into the starry night. There was a moment's silence before a rainbow of colours filled the sky above them.

The children woke and cheered the fireworks, and the men — filled with beer and wine — joined them.

Bonita bounced up to the boy and leant against him, her soft fur warming his leg. Feeling her tremble slightly at the noisy explosions, he stroked her gently and she relaxed at his touch.

As the smoke cleared, and the crowd waited expectantly for the next volley of fireworks, Albertino noticed a tiny star glow a little more brightly in the black sky.

'Happy birthday, Apu,' he said quietly.

Acknowledgements

This book would not be in your hands if not for the following people:

The social workers, psychiatrists and teachers who believed that art could help children deal with the trauma of war. *They Still Draw Pictures*, a collection of drawings by children from all parts of Spain, gave me a unique and inspiring insight into life before, during and after the civil war.

The readers, reviewers and writers of Authonomy.com who encouraged me past the first few chapters. In particular Andrew, Fred, Steve, Geffordson, Jake, B Worm, Jeff, Mary, Jane and, by association, Judy Chilcote.

Diana Beaumont, my agent, who refused to give up on Alberto and me, despite the bumps in the road.

My publisher Sam Humphreys, who remembered this story, found it a nurturing home at Mantle, and held my hand through every edit.

All the friends and family who always believed this novel would be published.

John, who gave me all the loving support I needed and a surname that fits on the cover.

My parents Val and Tony who, through many happy family holidays, helped me fall in love with Spain.

Acknowledgements

María Luisa, whose big laugh and warm generosity always made our family feel at home in Spain, and her husband Pascual, now sadly passed. A gardener and man of few words, Pascual left an indelible impression on my seven-year-old self, who, like Tino, couldn't imagine a life without a birthday. Without him, neither this book nor Alberto would ever have existed.